TIME
Tracers

THE STOLEN
SUMMERS

ALSO BY ANNABETH BONDOR-STONE AND CONNOR WHITE

THE SHIVERS! SERIES

WITHDRAWN

TIME TRACERS

THE STOLEN SUMMERS

BY ANNABETH BONDOR-STONE AND CONNOR WHITE

HARPER
An Imprint of HarperCollins Publishers

Library of Congress Cataloging-in-Publication Data
Names: Bondor-Stone, Annabeth, author. | White, Connor, author.
Title: Time tracers / by Annabeth Bondor-Stone and Connor White.
Description: First edition. | New York, NY : Harper, an imprint of
   HarperCollinsPublishers, [2018] | Summary: Seventh-grader Taj Butler is a champion time-waster,
but when his summer break is stolen by time thieves he is determined to get it back.
Identifiers: LCCN 2017034541 | ISBN 978-0-06-267142-4 (hardcover)
Subjects: | CYAC: Time--Fiction. | Robbers and outlaws--Fiction. | Adventure and adventurers--
Fiction. | Science fiction.
Classification: LCC PZ7.1.B665 Tim 2018 | DDC [Fic]--dc23
LC record available at https://lccn.loc.gov/2017034541

Typography by Brenda E. Angelilli
18 19 20 21 22 CG/LSCH 10 9 8 7 6 5 4 3 2 1
❖
First Edition

for robbie and julien

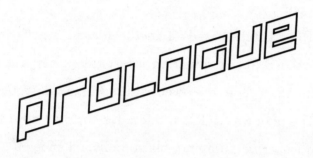

PROLOGUE

The party was over. The birthday girl was in tears.

"But it just started!" she wailed.

The creature was already on the move. It darted around the pile of presents stacked on the kitchen table, then brushed past the balloons, nearly popping one with its antennae. It leaped out of a window, into the front yard, and hit the ground running.

But the man in the gray suit was waiting.

"Don't move," he said, pulling out a small silver weapon.

The creature bared its needle-sharp teeth. Then it tore off in the other direction as fast as its six legs could go. It had to get to the boss. Failure was not an option.

The man was quick, though. He sprinted after the creature, arms pumping, black, polished shoes a blur against the sidewalk.

The creature looked back over its shoulder. The man was getting closer. It had to make a move. It darted into a busy street, weaving through traffic. A semitruck headed straight for it, too fast to outrun and too big to avoid. The creature crouched down low as the truck drove right over it. The enormous wheels just missed the creature's oily green shell. It skittered across two more lanes and made it safely to the other side.

Having shaken the man, the creature bolted down a dark alley to a big metal door. It checked to make sure it was alone. There was no sign of anyone. The creature banged on the door and it swung open.

The boss was standing in the shadowy doorway. "How much did you get?" he asked.

The creature whispered, "An hour. Maybe two."

"It's not enough. Get back out there," the boss sneered. Then he slammed the door in the creature's face.

The creature turned to go.

But standing at the other end of the alley was the man in the gray suit.

This time, there was nowhere to run.

The man wiped the sweat from his brow. He aimed his weapon. And then he fired.

CHAPTER 1

2:50 P.M.

Taj Carter was almost free. In just ten minutes, seventh grade would be over. Summer vacation was so close he could taste it—and it tasted like pizza. He squirmed in his desk. Ten measly minutes. He could handle that!

Monday through Friday for the past ten months, he had been forced from his warm, cozy bed, stuffed with cereal, and shuttled off to school for seven straight hours. That's 1,260 hours of school! So he could make it through ten more minutes ... right?

Wrong!

His teacher, Ms. Ludgate, was making it impossible. She had decided to spend the final class of the year droning on about the proper use of the semicolon. The boredom was crushing. Every second was an eternity. Out of the corner of his eye, Taj could see that his two best friends, Jen and Lucas, weren't doing much better than he was. Jen gnawed at the end of her pencil, her eyes glued to the clock. Taj watched a bead of sweat make its way down Lucas's round, freckled face.

Taj reviewed his options. Another trip to the water fountain? Ms. Ludgate would see right through that. Fake an illness? No. The school nurse hadn't trusted him since he told her that the class pet gave him "Gerbil Flu." He had no choice but to sit and wait.

Unless . . .

"Ms. Ludgate! Stop!" Taj shot his hand in the air.

Ms. Ludgate spun around from the whiteboard and spat her lemon candy in the trash can, but her face stayed as sour as ever. "What is it, Taj?"

"We forgot"—he thought fast—"the awards! The annual Taj awards!"

Ms. Ludgate crossed her arms. "Annual?"

"*First* annual!" Taj replied, bounding to the front of the room and leaping onto her desk. He grabbed a piece of paper and rolled it up to use as a microphone. The students rubbed their sleepy eyes and lifted their heads for ... whatever this was.

"Ladies and gentle-germs, it's been a long, long, *long* year. So let's take a moment to recognize all the great work we've done in this very classroom."

"Taj—" Ms. Ludgate tried to interrupt.

"This will only take a second!" He plowed ahead. "The first Taj award is for the Craziest Homework Excuse. And the winner is ..."

Jen and Lucas, always happy to be Taj's accomplices, started a drumroll on their desks.

"Tessa Peters!—whose essay on the American Revolution was 'accidentally taken by her dad when he went to go colonize Mars.' Hope Mr. Peters makes it back to Earth safely!"

Taj winked at Tessa and the whole class clapped wildly. Even Ms. Ludgate's permanently puckered lips twisted into something that looked like a smile.

Taj continued, "Next up is the Attendance Award. This year's winner, in a landslide, is Eric Wilson, who was on the class list but didn't show up for a single day of school because his family moved to South America last summer. Congratulations, Eric, wherever you are!"

As the class cheered, Ms. Ludgate stepped forward. "Okay, Taj, enough. I still have to give out your summer reading assignment."

"You got it, Ms. L!" He turned back to the class. "There's just one more award to give out today. It's the one you've all been waiting for . . . Loudest Bodily Noise!"

Everyone in the class busted out laughing. Ms. Ludgate opened her mouth to protest, but Taj pressed on.

"The competition was tight this year, especially since the cafeteria added 'Bean Fiesta' to the menu, but there can only be one winner. This year's prize goes to my good buddy Lucas, for when he found a mouse under his desk during allergy season, then screamed and sneezed at the same time!"

The class erupted into applause. Lucas stood up and took a bow. Taj chanted, "Scream-sneeze!" over and over again until the whole class joined him, while Lucas did a little victory dance.

"All right, enough," Ms. Ludgate interrupted. "Thank you, Taj. That was ... enlightening." She cleared her throat. "I still haven't given out your summer reading assignment. So, here it is—"

But before she could utter another word, the classroom was filled with the most beautiful sound in the world: the last bell of the year. The students sprang from their chairs, shrieking in delight, and threw their papers in the air like confetti.

"Where did the time go?!" Ms. Ludgate asked, looking around in confusion.

But the students didn't stop to help her figure it out. They stampeded out the door as fast as they could.

"Wait! Your summer reading assignment!" Ms. Ludgate shouted after them, but it was too late. The classroom was empty.

Taj ran through the hallway. He did it. He survived. Seventh grade was over. He was free! Free! FREE!!

He found Jen and Lucas at the lockers, emptying out their binders directly into the trash.

"Dude! That was awesome!" Lucas said.

"Agreed." Jen nodded. "Expertly done."

Taj shrugged. "I do what I can."

No one appreciated Taj's time-wasting talents more than Jen and Lucas. The three of them had been inseparable since their second grade field trip to the science museum, when they snuck onto the space shuttle and tried to launch it into orbit. (They would have, too, if it wasn't out of fuel.) They always had so much fun together that every weekend flew by. It was the only downside of hanging out with Taj—every day seemed to be a few hours short. But now they had a whole summer ahead of them.

And this was going to be the most epic summer ever.

Jen pressed her fingers to her forehead and scrunched up her face. "Locker combo . . . forgotten!" she declared then shut the door with a satisfying slam.

Taj knew that as much as she might want to, Jen could never really forget her locker combination. Her brain was like an encyclopedia. She held the high score on every video game because she memorized the cheat codes. She liked everything perfectly organized. The books in her bedroom were sorted alphabetically and her clothes were always color coordinated. Lucas, on the other hand, was the opposite. He usually had stains on his shirt and could barely remember his own birthday. But he was also the nicest guy in the whole school. He was always the first to introduce himself to a new kid or laugh at someone else's joke. Even though they were so different, they complemented each other perfectly. Like peanut butter and jelly—or, as Lucas preferred, peanut butter, jelly, bananas, and a splash of hot sauce.

Taj didn't waste any time getting down to business. "Okay, guys, summer planning meeting starts now. Let's cover the three major categories of fun: Spills, Chills, and Thrills. Lucas, what've you got for us?"

Lucas took a deep breath and said, "Major news from the Spills department, a.k.a. anything that can be spilled, a.k.a. all food-and-drink-related activity, a.k.a., I've spent the whole year thinking about this."

"Enough with the a.k.a.s!" Jen said.

Lucas grabbed three enormous bottles of root beer from the back of his locker and passed them out. "Drink up!" he said. "We've got to get our stomachs in shape for the next two months. Start expanding!" They all took a big slurp. Then Lucas continued, "I've already started planning this year's 'Roni Games, where we'll see who can eat the most pepperoni and macaroni. Once again, the committee has banned Rice-A-Roni because ... that stuff's just gross."

Taj cocked his head. "And who's the committee?"

Lucas pointed to himself and smiled. "This guy."

"Great work," Taj said. Then he turned to Jen. "What about the Chills?"

Jen pushed her thick brown hair behind her ears and said, "As always, we're looking to maximize chill time, people. My dad just got a new flat screen for the basement. I'm trying to convince him to mount it on the ceiling so we don't even have to sit up."

"Excellent," said Taj. "I made buttons to remind us to stay as lazy as humanly possible." He handed them out and pinned one to his T-shirt.

"Why do they say 'button'?" Lucas asked.

"They say *'butt on*,'" Taj explained. "Every time you look at it, you need to get your butt on something. Preferably a couch."

"Wow. Butt-on buttons," Jen marveled. "Taj, you've taken chilling to a whole new level."

Taj smiled with pride. "Now, as head of the Thrills department, I made three reservations for Indoor Sky-diving and got us early bird passes for the Gut Punch ride at Hurly World."

Lucas almost choked on his soda. "The new roller coaster? That thing is supposed to break your brain in half! How did you get passes?"

Taj shrugged. "They're way cheaper before the safety tests are done."

"Very smart," Jen said. "And where are we with the school-wide water fight?"

"Invitations have already been sent out. I'm just waiting for the industrial-strength water balloons. They're being shipped from Brazil," said Taj.

"Yes!" Lucas cheered.

"But wait, there's more!" Taj said in his best game show host voice. He reached into his backpack and pulled out a big rolled-up piece of paper. "May I present . . . The Map of Awesomeness!" He unrolled the paper, revealing an elaborate hand-drawn map of San Francisco that pinpointed all the most fun places in the city. Taj had been working on The Map of Awesomeness since September. It was color coded by category, with detailed notes on everything from the bowling alley hours to the name of the concession guy at the movie theater who always gave you a large popcorn even if you only paid for a medium. Taj had even highlighted the fastest way to get to each place so they could squeeze as much fun as possible into every single day.

"It's . . . beautiful," Jen whispered.

Lucas grinned. "I don't want to jinx it, but I think our hard work is going to pay off!"

Taj spit in his hand and held it up. "Best summer ever?"

"Best summer ever!" Jen and Lucas said, and spit in their hands, too.

Then they all high-fived. It was awesome—and disgusting.

On the way home, Taj stopped to pick up his little sister, Zoe, from preschool.

When she saw him, her face lit up. "Taj attack!" she shouted, leaping onto his legs and giggling uncontrollably.

"Hey, mini monster!" said Taj. "What'd you learn in school today?"

Zoe shrugged. "I don't remember."

Taj laughed.

Zoe was basically the cutest little sister ever. Imagine a kitten cuddling with a koala while sipping hot cocoa . . . She was cuter than that. She had big smiling eyes and a mess of curly hair that bounced like a thousand tiny Slinkys when she walked.

"Taj, will you do the hamster?" Zoe pleaded.

"Okay," he sighed. "Just once."

He took a deep breath and then contorted his face into a perfect imitation of a hamster. He stuck his tongue between his teeth and filled his cheeks with air so that they puffed like marshmallows. He bulged his eyes as far out as they would go, and then crossed them to make the hamster look stupendously silly.

Zoe collapsed into a fit of laughter. Taj's hamster impression was her favorite thing in the whole world. For a long time, it was the only thing that could make her smile. When Zoe was born, one of the valves in her heart wasn't fully developed. She had to have two surgeries, and the second one led to some complications that forced her to live in a hospital room for months.

Taj tried his best not to think about that time. His mom had been a walking zombie. She had been so worried about Zoe she could barely bring herself to speak to anyone. His dad had bunkered himself in his home office and buried himself in work. But Taj was determined not to let all the sadness infect his little sister like another sickness. They say laughter is the best medicine. Taj wasn't sure if that was true, but it was the only medicine he could prescribe. Whenever he visited her, he spent every moment telling jokes, doing silly dances, and, of course, making the hamster face.

"Are you excited for summer?" Taj asked, grabbing Zoe's backpack from her cubby. This was her first real summer vacation. Last year, she was still recovering from her surgeries, and before that, she was too little to understand that summer was, by far, the best season.

"Maybe," she said.

"Maybe?! Zoe, summer is the greatest stretch of time known to mankind! You can do whatever you want!" He grabbed her hand and they walked down the street toward their house. "Alice's Ice Cream gives out free samples. So you and I are going to try—hang on, let me do the math . . . ten thousand flavors!"

Zoe let out a delighted shriek.

Taj continued, "Every Friday, Dad's boss, Mr. Diaz, hosts a barbecue that's BYOB."

"What's that?"

"Bring Your Own Burger! And on Sundays, Coach Fig has a lawn bowling tournament. He's one of the cool teachers." They stopped at a corner and waited for the light to change. Taj pointed up at the street sign. "The school-wide water balloon fight is right here on Crescent Street. I got you a poncho." As they walked up the street, they passed the park. "I almost forgot the Fourth of July picnic!" Taj exclaimed. "I shouldn't even say anything. You wouldn't believe it if I did. The pie-eating contest, the potato sack race ... And to top it all off you get to light a bunch of stuff on fire!"

"Really?" Zoe's eyes widened.

"Trust me. Three hundred and sixty-four days a year people tell you, don't cause any explosions. Then one day, the rules go out the window! Zoe, you've got a lot of summers ahead of you, but you've got to make each one the best one ever. Cram as much fun as possible into every minute. Master every game you learned at recess. Make every daydream a reality. Because summer is the most precious thing on the entire planet!"

As Taj opened the gate to their front yard, he noticed some sand in Zoe's hair. "Did you play in the sandbox today?"

"No," she replied.

He mussed her hair and as soon as his fingers touched the sand—

He felt dizzy.

His neck prickled with goose bumps.

His whole body surged with heat.

He saw a bright flash of light and then a crystal clear image flooded his mind—like a memory, but it wasn't anything he had ever experienced. He was on the playground at Zoe's preschool, surrounded by her classmates. The teacher, Miss Allison, tossed a stone onto a chalk-lined grid on the ground, then jumped from one square to the next. She was teaching the class how to play hopscotch.

And all at once, the image was gone. Taj regained his balance. The heat dissolved.

"Look!" Zoe called from up ahead. "I remember what I learned in school today!" She picked up a pebble and tossed it onto the brick walkway, then hopscotched toward the front door.

Taj blinked a few times. He couldn't believe what he was seeing.

What just happened?

"OW!" Zoe howled. She had tripped on her shoelaces.

The door swung open and there was Mom. "Are you all right, sweetie?" she asked, scooping Zoe up.

"She's fine," said Taj. He hated how his parents still worried over every little thing, even though Zoe wasn't sick anymore.

"I want to play!" Zoe said, already giggling again.

"Okay," Mom said, putting her down with a smile. But then she spotted Zoe's untied shoelaces. "Taj, how many times do I have to ask you to teach her how to tie her shoes?"

"Can't *you* teach her?" said Taj.

"No. She wants her big brother to teach her."

"Mom, I tried!" he groaned. "But it took forever just to explain how to make one loop!"

"Well then, try harder! When things are difficult you can't just ignore them. Look what happens."

"She's *fine*," he repeated.

"That's not the point," said Mom. "I know that teaching a four-year-old how to tie her shoes isn't the most fun thing in the world, but she needs you."

Taj thought for a second. "I've got an idea! I'll go buy her some Velcro shoes!"

Mom's face softened and she couldn't help but laugh. "You're a piece of work," she said, shaking her head. "By the way, a package arrived for you this afternoon. Something from Brazil?"

"My water balloons!" Taj shouted, running into the house.

"Pace yourself!" she called after him. "You've got a big summer ahead of you!"

|||||||||||||||||||||||||||||||||||||||||||||||

That night, Taj was simmering with excitement. He added a few finishing touches to The Map of Awesomeness and rolled it up. Then, when he was sure no one was looking, he gave it a little hug. He climbed under the covers and closed his eyes, trying to force himself to sleep so he could wake up ready to start the summer. And with visions of water balloon fights floating in his head, he drifted off in no time.

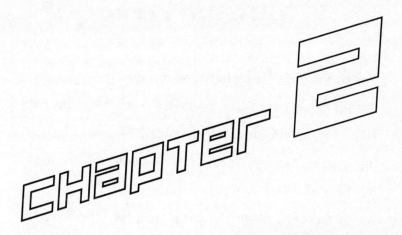

CHAPTER 2

7:35 A.M.

A pounding on Taj's bedroom door jolted him awake.

"Taj! Get up!" his mom shouted. "You're going to be late!"

He turned over and rubbed his eyes. "For what?" he called out groggily.

Mom yelled back, "For your first day of school!"

Taj sat up in bed and shook the sleep out of his brain. *What did Mom just say?*

The pounding on his door continued. "Taj! Hurry!

The bus is going to be here any minute!"

Taj rolled out of bed, padded across the room, and swung open the door. "Very funny," he said, brushing by her. "Did you buy chocolate chips? I'm making pancakes!"

He breezed down the stairs and into the kitchen, where Zoe and his dad were already sitting at the table. Dad had the newspaper open in front of his face so Taj could only see the top of his shiny bald head.

Mom followed quickly behind him. "You don't have time for breakfast!"

Taj grabbed the pancake mix from the pantry and set it on the counter. "Mom, I get that you're trying to mess with me. But it's the first day of summer, I have all the time in the world!"

"This isn't a joke, Taj!" she exploded. "Summer is over! You have to get to school!"

"Listen to your mother," Dad said sharply from behind the newspaper.

That's when Taj noticed something that sent the

room spinning—the date splashed across the front page of the paper was MONDAY SEPTEMBER 5.

"What?!" Taj stormed across the kitchen and tore the paper from Dad's hands.

"Excuse me!" He let out a very dadlike huff.

Taj flipped through the pages, certain that he was seeing things, but the date was unmistakable. "How is this possible?! Summer just started!"

Dad shrugged. "You know what they say. Time flies when you're having fun."

Taj dropped the paper and it fluttered to the floor.

"Either that, or the roller coaster shook the brains right out of you." Dad chuckled, pointing to a picture on the refrigerator.

Taj ripped the picture off the fridge and held it up to his face. In the photo, he was with Jen and Lucas, screaming his brains out on the Gut Punch coaster at Hurly World. He shook his head. He didn't remember going to Hurly World. He didn't remember anything about the summer. Sure, time flies when you're having fun. Everyone knows that. But this was different. His whole summer had just . . . disappeared.

At that moment, Zoe flipped over her cereal bowl, spilling milk and soggy Cheerios all over the floor. She pounded her tiny fists on the table and shouted, "I WANT A BEDTIME STORY!!!"

"Zoe, it's *morning*," Mom sighed, crouching down to clean up the mess.

Dad shook his head. "She's been saying weird things since she woke up." Then a puzzled look came over his face. "Come to think of it, I want a bedtime story, too."

"What is going on in this house today?" Mom said, exasperated. Then she pointed sharply at Taj. "Clothes. Backpack. Bus stop. *Now*."

Taj showed up at the bus stop, still in a fog. The scene there was grim. It looked like all the kids in the neighborhood were waiting to be shuttled to Siberia for a life sentence of hard labor. Jen and Lucas stumbled over. Jen was so bewildered she couldn't speak, and Lucas was sporting a scowl so deep it looked like his eye-brows were about to swallow his face.

For a brief second, Taj felt relieved. He might not be alone in this. They all looked at each other, dumb-founded, like they had a secret they were too scared to share. Then Taj broke the silence. "Dudes, where did our summer go?"

"I can't remember a single thing that happened!" Lucas said, throwing his hands up.

"But it *did* happen," Jen said, stupefied. "I checked the basement this morning. It was trashed. Candy wrappers under the cushions . . . popcorn kernels in the carpet . . . I saw three butt grooves in the couch." She looked Taj straight in the eye. "And they're deep, Taj. They're deep."

Lucas kicked the ground. "I don't even remember winning the 'Roni Games."

"You won the 'Roni Games?" Taj asked.

Jen muttered, "Of course he did. He always wins."

"I found the gold medal on my doorknob this morning but I still feel like I've been robbed," Lucas said darkly. Just then, his stomach let out a loud, low rumble. "Plus, I'm starving! I was so confused this morning that I forgot to eat breakfast!"

Jen and Taj looked at each other in shock. Lucas had never left the house without having at *least* one breakfast.

The school bus lumbered up the street and stopped in front of them. The doors squeaked open and let out an unwelcoming hiss.

"I can't believe we have to go back to school," Jen said, looking like she was about to puke. As she trudged up the steps and onto the bus, Taj noticed something even more unbelievable than Lucas skipping a meal. Jen was wearing mismatched socks—one with red stripes and one with blue polka dots.

Taj was the last on, and the doors snapped shut behind him like prison gates. The students onboard looked miserable. Way more miserable than if this was just a normal miserable first day of school.

As the bus rolled down the street, Taj stared out the window. The whole neighborhood seemed—*off*—somehow, but he couldn't put his finger on it. When they drove past the park, he saw a whole family dressed in red, white, and blue, holding sparklers and American flags like they were there for the Fourth of July picnic . . . but they were two months late. When the bus stopped at the corner, Taj saw Dad's boss, Mr. Diaz, standing on his front lawn, staring blankly at his barbecue. On the grill was a burger so charred it looked like it had been cooking for three days.

Taj elbowed Jen. "What is going *on* today?"

Jen shook her head. "I'm just glad we're going home."

Lucas spun around. "Um, news flash! We're going *to* school."

"Oh . . . right," she said. Then she buried her head in her hands. "This is *terrible.*"

The bus arrived at school and everyone flooded out. Across the street, Taj spotted something seriously strange going on inside Alice's Ice Cream. Alice was at the glass door, wearing a bathrobe, flipping the welcome sign from Open to Closed over and over again, unable to decide which one was true.

Then Taj heard it—the first bell of the year. Also known as the *worst* bell of the year. School was starting, and there was nothing he could do about it.

The morning dragged like a slug on a hot sidewalk. History class seemed to last as long as the Dark Ages. Every minute of science was dissected into sixty endless seconds. Taj didn't understand a single thing that was happening in French, but that's because he had stumbled into the wrong room on his way to Spanish class.

No matter how hard he tried, he couldn't focus with all the questions clouding his mind: *Where did the summer go? Why can't I remember a single thing that happened? And why is everyone acting like they took one too many soccer balls to the head?*

And then there was gym class.

"LET'S GO, PEOPLE! LINE UP!" Coach Fig shouted from under the basketball hoop. He blew his whistle and everyone gathered at the sideline.

"Everyone knows PE is the most fun class in the entire school. And I intend to keep it that way!"

The whole class cheered.

"Except for today. Because we're doing Fitness Testing. Starting with wind sprints."

The whole class groaned.

Lucas's eyes rolled so far back he could almost see his brain. There was nothing he hated more than running for no reason—except running for no reason in front of an audience. Every year was the same. PE started off with Fitness Testing, and Lucas was always the slowest person in the whole class. It was the kind of humiliation that took months to shake. "I can't do it. Not again," he muttered.

Taj patted him on the shoulder. "It's only a few seconds."

Jen piped up, "Sprint your heart out just this once,

then you can rest easy until high school!"

Coach Fig pulled a stopwatch out of his shorts pocket. "You're up first, Ailsworth."

Lucas sighed and dragged himself to the starting line.

"More like *Snails*-worth!" one of the students shouted.

Taj caught Lucas's eye and mouthed, *"You can do it."*

Lucas put his foot on the line, crouched down, and took a deep breath.

"On your mark...get set...GO!" Coach Fig shouted, starting the stopwatch.

Lucas tore off across the gym. He swung his arms wildly and pumped his legs. When he reached the wall, he turned around and sprinted back even faster. Taj hadn't seen Lucas run this fast since they accidentally knocked over a wasps' nest in his backyard. Lucas's face glowed bright red and he was panting like a snow dog at the end of a thirty-mile sled race. He crossed the finish line, threw his arms in the air, and collapsed on the floor.

Coach Fig stopped the timer. "Seven hours and two minutes."

"*WHAT?!*" Lucas screamed from the floor.

Everyone in the class burst out laughing.

"I know I'm slow, but I'm not *that* slow!" Lucas huffed.

"Sorry, buddy. Better luck next year," Coach Fig said.

Taj knew he had to say something. It would take Lucas the rest of his life to live this down.

"Coach, that's impossible!" Taj called out. "Check your stopwatch again!"

Coach Fig held the stopwatch up to his face. "Eighteen seconds?! That can't be right! It just said seven hours! And that sprint took all day!" he sputtered. He looked around at the class like he was waiting for some sort of explanation, but no one knew what to say. And that's when Coach Fig *really* lost it. He threw the stopwatch on the ground and shouted, "It's broken! I just bought the dumb thing yesterday! Or . . . was it a year ago? It doesn't matter! What a hunk of junk!" He jumped up and down on the stopwatch, crushing it into tiny plastic pieces.

From the back of the gym, Katie Wertheim, the quietest girl in school, raised her hand and said in her high-pitched voice, "Coach Fig? Are you okay?"

Coach Fig shouted at the ceiling, "I'M JUST SO TIRED!" He dropped to his knees. "You know what? Do whatever you want. Climb the rope! Do a chin-up! Play tug-of-war! I don't care!" He pulled up the hood of his sweatshirt and yanked the drawstrings so tight that his face nearly disappeared inside. "GOOD NIGHT!" he screamed. Then he slumped over onto the floor and fell asleep.

There was a long silence. Then Katie squeaked, "Is he . . . *dead*?"

Taj scooted over to Coach to check on him. "He's fine. He's just . . . napping." He glanced at his classmates' faces, stricken with confusion. "I'm sure everything's going to be okay," he said, though he didn't quite believe that himself. This was shaping up to be the weirdest first day of school ever. There was only one thing he could think to do. He flung open the equipment closet door, grabbed a giant bucket of red rubber balls, and tossed them into the gym. Then he shouted, "Dodgeball fight!"

The students leaped to their feet. No one was going to pass up a chance at a dodgeball free-for-all. And Coach Fig *had* given them permission to do whatever they wanted. As the balls bounced around the room, the fun was contagious. Coach Fig slept as soundly as a baby while streaks of red flew above his head and ricocheted off the walls. Laughter echoed through the room as people pelted each other left and right. There were no rules, and no one cared. Jen grabbed two dodgeballs then scurried up the climbing rope to launch an aerial attack. Lucas got hit hard, but the ball bounced off his stomach right back at the kid who threw it. Taj jumped and twisted as a ball whizzed right under him. As he landed, he saw another ball hurtling toward him. He flinched and covered his face, bracing himself for the impact.

The ball was just inches from his nose, when all of a sudden—

It froze in midair.

All of the wild screams suddenly stopped and the gym went silent.

Taj turned slowly and saw Jen's arm stretched out in front of her. A dodgeball hovered at her fingertips, held up by . . . nothing. Lucas was frozen in place, and so was the ball that had just bounced off his belly. It was like someone had pressed the pause button on the whole school. Everyone was stuck in suspended animation except for Taj. The only sound was his own heavy breathing. He took a step forward but no one else moved. It was like he was suddenly in a wax museum.

And then, all at once, there was a deafening crash. Taj spun around to see a city bus plow through the gym wall in an explosion of concrete and metal.

Taj put his arms up to cover his face as the bus came to a screeching halt inches in front of him. The bus was big and bulky, with dingy white paint. The electronic sign above the windshield said Out of Service. The driver leaped out and ran toward Taj through the cloud of dust. He was a tall, broad-shouldered man wearing a steel-gray business suit. Taj backed up until he was pressed against the wall.

The man held up his hand. "It's okay, Taj."

"Wh-who are you?" Taj stammered.

"My name is Eon. I'm a Time Tracer," he said. "Your summer was stolen. And if you want to get it back, I need you to come with me."

CHAPTER 3

1:07 P.M.

Taj could barely speak. He felt like his head had been stuffed in a washing machine that was stuck on spin cycle.

He cleared his throat and said, "My summer was *stolen*?!"

Eon nodded. "And not just yours. Everyone you know had their summers stolen, too. You may have noticed people acting a little strange today."

Taj's mind flashed to Jen's mismatched socks; Lucas skipping breakfast; Zoe begging for a bedtime story first thing in the morning. And he looked over at Coach Fig, curled up on the floor with his sweatshirt over his head. "A *little*?" he shouted.

"That's because they had too much time stolen at once. It's called TTD—Total Time Deprivation."

"Okay, dude, I don't know what your deal is. You seem super official with the nice suit and everything. But people can't steal time!"

"Not people," said Eon, his eyes flickering around the gym like he was looking at something that Taj couldn't see. "Time thieves."

"What are—?"

"Put these on," said Eon, shoving a pair of wire-rimmed glasses into Taj's hands.

Taj placed the glasses on his face and was horrified at what he saw—Bugs. Giant ones. Scurrying down the walls of the gym. They had black bulbous bodies the size of beach balls and long, hairy legs. They looked like oversized spiders. He whipped the glasses off— and the creatures were gone. Then he put the glasses back on and there they were again, but closer this time. "Whoa! Spooky glasses, man." Taj shuddered. "What is this, virtual reality?"

"No," Eon said flatly.

Just then, one of the time thieves ran straight toward Taj. Eon took out a small silver weapon and pulled the trigger. With an earsplitting crack, an electrified blue net shot out of the barrel, trapping the thief. Through the glasses, Taj saw the net squeeze the thief until it popped like a balloon. Taj felt the wet, gooey guts splatter all over his face. This wasn't virtual reality; this was very, very real. He screamed and bolted under the bleachers.

Eon covered him, launching blue nets with expert precision, obliterating time thieves left and right all around Taj. CRACK! POP! CRACK! POP! Taj watched in disbelief as one made its way up the climbing rope to nearly where Jen was dangling, but right before it reached her shoes, Eon blasted it.

Taj shouted over the din, "Did the time thief things

put everyone on pause?"

"No, that was me," Eon called back. "I couldn't let them steal more time so I froze it. It'll help protect your friends, but it makes the thieves really, *really* angry."

Suddenly, two more time thieves skittered out from behind the scoreboard and descended onto the bleachers. "A little help!" Taj yelled, scurrying out from under the lowest bench.

"Get to the bus! You'll be safe in there!"

Taj sprinted toward the city bus that had crashed into the gym. He sidestepped a row of back-to-school backpacks and brushed past Katie Wertheim's long blond ponytail, which was sticking straight out behind her head. But just as he was about to reach the bus, a time thief leaped out of nowhere and landed right in front of him. It was so close he could see its glossy green eyes.

"NOT GONNA HAPPEN!" Taj screamed. He skidded to a stop, turned on his heels, and ran at full speed in the opposite direction.

He burst through the gym doors and into the hallway. It was deserted except for Vice Principal Eggbert, who was frozen in place scolding some poor sixth grader who was probably just late for class. Taj dropped to the floor and slid between Eggbert's legs. He was not slowing down—for anything. He could hear one of the time thieves getting closer, hissing and snarling at him. Taj spotted an open locker. He flung the metal door backward and the thief collided into it.

"Take that, you oversized raisin!" Taj shouted, pumping his fist. But then he saw a dozen more heading his way. Taj sprinted as fast as he could, desperate to find an exit. As he passed by classrooms, he could see that everyone in the whole school was frozen in place. Teachers stood still at the whiteboards. Students in the art room had become statues. The school nurse was stuck in the middle of applying a Band-Aid to a kid's scraped knee.

Taj darted into the cafeteria, which was full of seventh graders paused in the middle of lunch. They held half-eaten sandwiches up to their mouths. Milk cartons and plastic trays were strewn about the tables. Taj hid behind a giant trash can. When he heard a door swinging open, he peered out and was relieved to see that it was Eon.

"I told you to get on the bus!" Eon said.

"Sorry! I was just trying to get away from the *man-eating bugs!*"

"Those are time thieves. Not bugs. And they don't eat people. They steal time," Eon said, sounding frustrated. "You ever wonder why time flies when you're having fun?"

"Yeah . . . ?" Taj nodded.

Eon crouched down next to him. "Well, guess what? It doesn't fly. It. Gets. Stolen."

"You've got to be kidding me." Taj balked.

Eon narrowed his icy blue eyes and clenched his square jaw. "Do I look like a comedian?"

As Taj tried to wrap his mind around what he was hearing, time thieves flooded into the cafeteria. They leaped onto the tables, knocking over the greasy food in their path. Eon pulled Taj down lower behind the trash can and readied his weapon.

Taj whispered, "So you're telling me that when I'm hanging out with my friends for hours and it feels like five minutes . . ."

"Time thieves," Eon said, firing off a deluge of blue nets. So many time thieves popped at once that it sounded like the end of a fireworks show. But still more flooded in through the doors.

"Birthday parties? Weekends?!" Taj said incredulously.

"Time thieves!" Eon shouted. He picked up the trash can and hurled it at the incoming swarm, squashing them all except for one. But it was a big one, with legs hairier than Coach Fig's. Eon aimed his weapon, but when he pulled the trigger, nothing happened. He was out of ammo. A flash of panic crossed his face as the time thief stampeded forward.

Without thinking, Taj grabbed the nearest soda

can, shook it up as hard as he could, and launched it, hitting the time thief right between the eyes. As the soda can exploded, so did the thief.

Eon dabbed the sweat from his forehead with a neatly pressed handkerchief. "Not bad," he said.

Taj tried to catch his breath. "What. Just. Happened?!"

Eon ignored the question. "Come on, let's get to the bus."

Taj held up his hands. "No way, dude! I wasn't running for my life until you showed up. No offense, but I'm not exactly looking to spend more quality time together."

"Taj, I've been a Time Tracer for twenty years. I've spent my whole life fighting time thieves. And I've never seen a whole summer get stolen—much less all the summers from an entire neighborhood. This is bad. Real bad."

"So what does this all have to do with me?"

"It'll all be explained. But first I need you to—"

"—get on the bus? No! Ever heard of a thing called Stranger Danger?"

Eon looked frustrated but he took a deep breath. "You can do this your way or you can do this my way, but there's only one way we're going to get those summers back. And that's if we work together."

Suddenly, there was a loud crash from the cafeteria kitchen. It sounded like a giant metal refrigerator had just tipped over. Taj saw a throng of time thieves crawling over the still-frozen lunch ladies, heading straight for him.

He whipped his head toward Eon and shouted, "Okay! Your way!"

Eon grabbed Taj's wrist and they ran as fast as they could back to the gym, the angry time thieves right behind them. He hoisted Taj onto the bus and slid into the driver's seat. He pulled a lever and the doors closed with a heavy slam like a bank vault sealing.

Now that Taj was onboard, he realized that this was definitely not a normal city bus. It only had three rows of seats behind the steering wheel. The rest had been ripped up to make room for a mobile command center. The insides of the windows housed giant computer screens. Each showed a bird's-eye view of a different area of the city. The images were dotted with glowing patches of red and orange. It looked a little like a weather map, but Taj had a sneaky feeling it wasn't tracking storms.

Eon kicked the bus into gear, turning the engine from a rumble to a roar.

THUD! THUD! THUD!

The time thieves flung themselves onto the outside of the bus. They pummeled the windows, scratching and clawing.

Eon stepped hard on the gas. The bus jolted backward with the force of a jet engine, throwing the time thieves into the air and scattering them across the gym. The bus zoomed back out of the giant hole it had made in the side of the building, crushing chunks of concrete beneath its wheels.

1:28 P.M.

As the bus peeled out onto the street, Taj could see through the windshield that outside of his school, life was normal. Time was unpaused. Dogs barked. Birds chirped. A bald guy in a business suit screamed into his cell phone. Traffic moved forward, and no one batted an eye at the out-of-service bus folding swiftly into the flow.

Taj sat down right behind the driver's seat. "Where are we going?"

"I'm taking you to meet F.T.," said Eon.

"F.T.?"

But Eon didn't explain. Instead, he held up his wrist and spoke into a large black watch. "Send in the Erasers. We need to restart time inside the school as soon as possible."

"Yes, sir," a voice responded.

That's when Taj saw three more identical out-of-service buses heading in the opposite direction. He could just glimpse that inside each one were men and women wearing bright white protective suits and bubble- shaped helmets.

"Who are they?" Taj asked.

"Erasers," said Eon. "They'll put your school back together exactly as it was before. When they're done, I'll restart time and no one will know that any of this ever happened."

"How can you stop and start time whenever you want?" Taj asked.

"With this." Eon showed Taj his watch. The precise time down to the nanosecond was displayed on the sleek glass face, and there were red buttons along the side.

"Whoa, cool!" said Taj. "Can I try it?!"

"*No.*"

Taj tried to picture the Erasers putting everything back together. They had a lot of work to do—repairing the giant hole in the wall, rearranging the dodgeballs, fixing the lunch ladies' hair nets ... That's when he realized that even if they managed to restore everything perfectly, there would still be one thing missing.

"Hey!" He leaped to his feet. "Isn't everyone going to notice I'm gone? If I'm not home for dinner, my mom is going to freak!"

"I've got you covered," Eon said, his eyes steadied on the road. He tapped his watch and the face lit up. "Put me through to the Banker."

A voice came through. "This is Skyler."

"I need a memory buffer around Taj Carter. District 220."

"You got it, Eon," she said quickly.

Eon tapped his watch again and it went dark.

"Banker?" asked Taj.

"Memory Banker," Eon explained. "She'll put memories of you into the minds of your teachers, your friends, your family, anyone who might miss you. That way they'll never fully notice that you're gone. You know that feeling like you just saw someone but you can't remember where?"

"Yeah . . ."

"That's a memory buffer."

"You can change people's memories?!" Taj's eyes lit up. "Hey, while you're in there, can you make it so Jen thinks *I* have the high score on *Doomsday Soccer III*? It's her favorite video game. That'll drive her insane!"

"No," said Eon.

"Hey, have you ever thought about saying yes once in a while?" Taj asked.

Eon thought for a moment. "No."

Eon wove the bus through the narrow streets of downtown San Francisco with the speed and precision of a race car driver. They passed pristine department stores and brightly painted town houses. Trolleys connected to cables clanged along like metal marionettes. Taj spotted the brick facade of the Giants baseball stadium. He thought back to a Saturday last spring when his dad took him to a game. He remembered how much fun they'd had and how the day seemed to pass in an instant. Now he knew why.

Eon pulled over in front of the San Francisco Ferry Building, a sprawling structure topped by a massive white clock tower.

"Here?" Taj asked skeptically. "This is where my mom always drags me to go shopping."

"Just follow me," said Eon.

The Ferry Building was bustling with people. Commuters raced by, their eyes glued to their phones, and tourists ambled along, oohing and aahing at the sailboats outside while nibbling on expensive cheese. The air smelled sweet and Taj's stomach growled as he passed a glass case of chocolate-covered strawberries.

"Stay close," Eon said. He led Taj to an elevator bay where two women were waiting, their arms full of shopping bags. The elevator in front of them opened and the women shuffled on. Taj stepped forward to join them, but then he felt a soft tug on the back of his shirt.

"We'll get the next one," said Eon.

The women smiled at him and the elevator doors closed.

Eon glanced over his shoulder, scanning the area. When he saw that no one was around, he held his watch in front of the down button. There was a tiny flash of light, and then a *ding!* from the elevator at the very end of the bay. A sign that said Out of Service was taped to the doors, but they slid open without a sound.

"Wow! City buses! Out-of-service elevators! You're *fancy*," Taj quipped. "Let me guess—F.T. lives in a janitor's closet?"

Eon shot him a look as the doors shut behind them. This elevator didn't have any buttons, only a square glass pad.

"Hold on," Eon said, gripping the metal railing.

"I think I can handle an elevator ride," said Taj.

Eon shrugged. "Suit yourself."

He scanned his watch in front of the glass pad and all at once, the elevator plunged into a free fall. Taj screamed at the top of his lungs. His stomach felt like it was trying to crawl out of his throat. This was just like being on the Death Drop at Hurly World, except there didn't seem to be an end to this ride. They kept on going, lower and lower underground, until Taj was certain they were nearing the core of the Earth and would end up in a pool of molten lava. Meanwhile, Eon was totally unfazed. He even tapped his foot to the cheesy elevator music.

Then the elevator came to an abrupt stop and Taj crashed to the floor. He glared up at Eon and shouted, "A little *warning* would have been nice!"

"I said hold on," said Eon.

But before Taj could grab a handhold, the elevator flew forward like it had been shot out of a cannon.

"AHH!" Taj screamed as he was plastered against the back wall.

The elevator pivoted left—then forward—then right—then forward again. Taj bounced off the walls like he was a pinball.

Finally, they jolted to a halt. Taj lay on his back, groaning.

There was a soft *ding!* and the doors slid open. Standing there was a plump, middle-aged man with thinning hair and kind eyes. Like Eon, he was wearing a gray suit, but his had a gold pin on the lapel in the shape of a pendulum. He looked down at Taj and sighed. "Somebody didn't hold on." Then he smiled warmly. "Hello, Taj. My name is Father Time. But everyone calls me F.T." He reached out his hand and pulled Taj to his feet. "Welcome to the Universal Time Agency."

CHAPTER 5

2:04 P.M.

When Taj stepped out of the elevator, his jaw dropped. He was at the base of an enormous glass dome that was hundreds of stories high. It stretched out as far and wide as he could see. It was full of people rushing around, all dressed in gray suits, with black watches on their wrists. Suspended just below the shimmering ceiling was a ball of golden light as big as a hot air balloon. Even though they were deep underground, the ball lit up the whole place like a bright summer day. Smaller orbs floated around it, each its own stunning color—marbled blue, clay red, chalk white. It was as if Taj was looking at the solar system itself.

"This. Place. Is. Awesome!!!" he blurted out as he tried to take it all in. "Where am I?! Who built this?! How much glass cleaner do you guys go through?!" He pointed straight up above him. "Is that the *sun*?!"

"It's the whole solar system!" F.T. exclaimed. "Well, not the real one, but it's the best model we've got."

"Way better than the one I made for the science fair last year," said Taj. "That thing was mostly Silly Putty."

Running up the side of the colossal dome was a glass walkway with a silver-metal railing. Taj noticed that the people in the gray suits were beginning to gather along the walkway. There were hundreds of them . . . maybe thousands, stepping out from every doorway. They looked down at Taj, chattering and pointing.

Taj's face flushed like he'd been caught singing in the shower. "Who are all these people?"

"Time Tracers. Protectors of the clock." F.T. placed a hand on Taj's shoulder. "Time is the most precious and valuable resource in the world. It is our job to protect it. And we've been looking for you for a very long time."

Taj fidgeted. "Okay—but why am I here?"

"We believe you are very special, Taj. If our calculations are correct, you have powers no one has ever possessed before. You're the one we've been waiting for. The one who can return time," said F.T.

Taj was taken aback. "Return it?"

"To its rightful owners," F.T. said, looking at Taj expectantly. "Time is like a river. Since it first started flowing, it has only ever run in one direction. Until now." He turned to Eon. "Bring me the birthday party."

Eon nodded and rushed off.

Taj could feel the thousands of eyes watching his every move. "I ... I don't get it."

F.T. clasped his hands together and smiled. "May I borrow your shoelace?"

Before Taj could answer, F.T. was on the ground, untying Taj's shoe. He yanked the lace clean out then held it up in front of Taj. "Think of time as this shoelace. Normally, it travels in a straight line." He pulled the lace tight so it formed a straight line. "Let's say the left end is Saturday morning and the right end is Sunday evening. When time is stolen, it bends." He brought the plastic ends of the lace closer together, forming a semi-circle. "See how much closer they are now?"

"So that's why my weekends race by?" Taj said, transfixed.

"Exactly. But this summer, you made so many people have so much fun that when it all was stolen, this happened." He connected the two ends of the shoelace, forming a complete circle.

Taj shook his head. "I'm confused. I made a circle?"

"You created a portal." Father Time tied the ends in a knot. "We call it a Wormhole. And now, you have the ability to return time."

"Really?" Taj said.

"Well"—F.T. cleared his throat—"that's our theory.

And after centuries of searching, we're about to find out if it's correct."

Eon returned, holding a small glass test tube.

Taj felt the air around him thicken with anticipation. All of the Time Tracers fell silent. They leaned so far forward it looked like they might fall right over the railing. "No pressure, huh?" Taj gulped.

F.T. took the test tube from Eon and showed it to Taj. It was filled with tiny white granules that looked like sand. "This is stolen time. Every grain is a second." F.T. turned to Eon and asked, "Who does it belong to?"

"Caroline Thompson. Age seven," Eon responded. "Time thieves attacked her birthday party. Made the whole thing go by in the blink of an eye."

F.T. nodded. "Hold out your hand," he said to Taj. He unscrewed the lid and poured the sandy substance onto Taj's palm. Taj felt like he was standing center stage for a show he'd never rehearsed.

F.T. looked at the sand. Taj looked at F.T. Eon looked at Taj, his jaw clenched.

And then . . . nothing.

"What do I do?" Taj whispered.

F.T. whispered back, "I have no idea!"

Another moment passed. Just long enough for Taj to see Eon's gaze cast to the ground. The energy in the room deflated like a popped tire. The Time Tracers shook their heads and murmured to each other in hushed voices.

But then, just when he was about to pour the sandy time back into its container, Taj felt a rush of heat surge through him. The hairs on the back of his neck prickled. He felt light-headed. There was a ringing that began in his ears and somehow spread through his whole body.

The sand began to rise straight up, a thin line barely wider than a single grain, like an hourglass in reverse.

A brightness eclipsed Taj's vision like he'd just stared into the sun and—WHOOSH!—his mind was flooded with a series of vivid images. A cake with seven candles, a colorful piñata hanging from a tree, a stack of brightly wrapped presents. Taj felt the joy of a birthday party. His stomach growled as if he were waiting for his slice of cake. But it wasn't his party, it wasn't his house, these weren't his friends. Yet it felt like he was there and had always been there.

Taj's eyes snapped open just in time to see the narrow strand of time shoot up toward the sky and disappear. There was still quite a bit of sand left in Taj's hand, but F.T. didn't seem to care.

"Did you see that?" F.T. said breathlessly. "That was it. That must have been it!" He spun around and grabbed Eon by his suit jacket. "Eon, quick, check Caroline Thompson's time levels!"

Eon swiftly tapped the face of his watch. In the short time that Taj had known Eon, he had always had the same stony expression on his face, harder to read than a Russian textbook. Until now. His eyes widened and his mouth fell open. "He did it."

Father Time grabbed Taj's wrist and lifted his hand in the air. He looked up at the massive crowd of onlookers and shouted, "He is the Worm!"

2:12 P.M.

A cheer went up from the Tracers that rattled the railing and echoed off the glass walls. Taj felt like he had just single-handedly won the Super Bowl, even though he still didn't understand what any of it meant.

"Why did you just call me a worm?" Taj asked.

"Not *a* worm. *The* Worm!" F.T. hopped up and down and clapped with excitement. "You're the only person who can return time through the Wormhole! Finding you is the single greatest discovery . . . well, of all time!"

Taj cocked his head. "And you couldn't think of a better name than *the Worm*?!"

"Well, have you really looked at a worm lately?" said F.T. "They're fascinating creatures. And so wiggly! Besides, it's not about what you're called, it's about what you can do. What you *have* to do. You are our only hope for returning those summers."

Eon stepped closer to F.T. and whispered, "Sir, we may have a problem. We gave him an entire birthday party and he only returned twelve seconds."

F.T. waved him aside. "Oh, Eon, don't be such a party pooper. It was his first try! He'll learn to hone his abilities." He patted Taj on the back. "Isn't that right?"

Taj honestly had no idea how he had returned the time or how he would be able to do it again. But he didn't want to disappoint Father Time. "Sure, I'm up for anything," he said. "As long as I don't have to ride that elevator again."

F.T. laughed. "We must get started." He raised up his hand and the Agency immediately fell silent. "Tracers! This is indeed a momentous occasion, but we have a lot of work to do and a lot of time to return. Everyone, back to your stations!"

With that, the throngs of people all held two fingers to their wrists, like some sort of military salute. And then, like clockwork, they returned to their posts. Eon turned and strode toward the long ramp that spiraled up the edge of the dome. F.T. motioned for Taj to follow.

As he hurried to catch up, Taj noticed a large, official-looking seal etched into the floor. It was an image of an hourglass with *Universal Time Agency* written above it, and below it, the words *Tempus Fugit*.

"What does that mean?" Taj asked as they hurried up the ramp.

F.T. explained, "It's Latin for *Time Flies*, a term first coined in the year 29 BCE. Time thieves have existed for as long as humanity, stealing fun time in order to live."

"But why only fun time? Why can't they take my time when I'm doing my homework?" Taj asked. "They can have as much of that as they want."

"Boring time doesn't help them live any longer. It's like how animals can live off plants and meat but not rocks and bark."

Taj was beginning to understand. "So stealing a boring Monday morning would be like . . ."

"Eating a brick. And nobody wants to eat a brick!" F.T. burst into a fit of laughter.

Taj couldn't help but laugh, too. F.T.'s warmth was infectious.

"We've been fighting time thieves for thousands of years." He placed his hand on Taj's shoulder. "And now finally, *finally*, we may be able to stop them once and for all."

Eon spun around. "Don't let it get to your head, Worm."

"That's *Mr.* Worm to you!" Taj shot back.

F.T. let out another hearty laugh. "I love this kid!"

As they walked, they passed dozens upon dozens of glass doors and long, winding hallways. Taj couldn't wrap his head around how huge the Agency was and couldn't even begin to imagine where all the miles of corridors led.

"How big is this place?" Taj asked.

"Big. And growing bigger every day," said F.T. "After all, the world is becoming a more fun place. Back in the Middle Ages when everyone was just trying their best not to catch the plague, the job was a breeze. Now we have to work around the clock to stay on top of all the fun." He pointed at a door that said Research and Development. "This is where we test new time crime-fighting technology. If you go in there, you might want to wear a hard hat."

At that moment, Taj heard a giant explosion on the other side of the door.

Eon frowned. "Maybe don't go in there."

As they rounded the bend, Taj had to stop and stare. Through a plate glass wall, he saw a massive training facility teeming with Tracers. But unlike everyone else in the building, they weren't wearing gray suits. They were dressed in black combat gear. Some were lined up at a shooting range, firing off weapons that Taj had never seen before. Others were sprinting on treadmills, oxygen masks over their mouths and wires attached to their chests, recording their vital signs.

"Special Ops," F.T. explained. "Investigators like Eon are the brains of any Time Tracing mission. Special Operatives are . . . well, they're the guts." He pointed to an area of the facility closed off by a chain-link fence. "That's Syd. One of the best."

Inside the fence was a muscular woman wearing big black headphones with a silver spiral on the side. She had closely cropped blond hair and a long, thin scar that ran from the corner of her left eye all the way down her cheek. She was engaged in hand-to-hand combat with a hairy, green-eyed time thief. She delivered a perfect roundhouse kick that sent it whizzing through the air. It collided with the fence so hard that Taj flinched.

"Don't worry," Eon said, "it's not a real thief. It's a bio-robotic training tool."

Maybe it wasn't real, but when it hurled itself into Syd's stomach, it still knocked the wind out of her. She clambered back to her feet, gritted her teeth, and grabbed it in a headlock until it popped, just like the time thieves did back at Taj's school.

She let out a guttural war cry, put her hands on her knees, and took a breath before raising her arm and shouting, "Again!"

A red light flashed, a warning sound blared, and another time thief descended from the ceiling. The whole exercise started all over.

"Whoa, cool!" Taj said, banging his hands against the glass. Syd whipped her head around and for a second it looked like she was about to stomp *him*. But then the corner of her mouth turned up into a grin. She cracked her knuckles and winked.

"Let's keep moving!" Eon called from up ahead.

When Taj and F.T. caught up, Eon scanned his watch in front of a set of double doors. The doors slid open, revealing a long hall of large offices with glass walls. Inside each one was a team of people working feverishly in front of giant screens. As he hustled down the hall, Taj noticed that everyone was glancing up from their stations to stare at him.

Eon and F.T. led Taj into an office that said District 220 on the door. There was a crew of about fifteen people inside. When they saw F.T., they saluted by holding two fingers to their wrists.

"Taj, meet your team. The District 220 Tracers," said F.T.

Eon added, "These people have been protecting you your entire life."

A guy wearing sandals with socks and a Hawaiian shirt under his suit jacket ran up to Taj. "Ernie Garcia. Head Pilot. It's a *real* honor." As soon as they shook hands, Ernie shouted, "The Worm touched my hand!"

"Enough," Eon said pointedly. "Any sign of the summers?"

"Nothing yet." Ernie sat down at a panel of high-tech joysticks. A giant screen in front of him showed an aerial view of a busy street. There were red-and-orange blotches scattered throughout, just like the screens on the bus windows.

"Wow!" Taj marveled. "This looks like the military designed a video game! Jen would be drooling all over it!"

"Please! No drooling!" said Ernie. "We don't want it to short-circuit. It took forever to build."

"What does it do?" said Taj.

Ernie grinned. "It hunts down fun." He jiggled one of the joysticks. "As Head Pilot, I steer the scanners, which are basically giant drones that fly over the city detecting fun time." He adjusted his glasses. "Once I find the fun, I send out Tracers to get there before the time thieves do. It's pretty cool stuff!" He glanced up at Taj. "I mean, not as cool as you, but—"

"Ernie," Eon warned.

"Sorry!" Ernie turned back to Taj. "Anyway, right now I'm using every scanner we have to search for those summers. I've scoured half the district already."

"Keep looking," said Eon. He walked over to a woman who was hunched in front of a computer connected to a giant metal data server. She was typing quickly with one hand while chugging from a thermos with the other.

"What's the status on the memory buffer, Skyler?" Eon asked.

Taj realized that this must be the Banker, who Eon had called from the bus.

She took a big slurp from her thermos then spoke faster than anyone Taj had ever heard. "Memory buffer is up and running! No one's gonna notice this kid is gone. But it wasn't easy. He knows a *lot* of people. By the way, you want some coffee? Does the kid want coffee? Do kids drink coffee? I don't know, I don't have any. Kids, that is. I have a *lot* of coffee."

Eon turned to Taj. "Skyler makes sure no one in the district is aware of the Agency."

Skyler shook her head. "Last weekend, three Time Tracers were trying to catch a time thief at a wedding and they fell through the skylight onto the dance floor. They *literally* crashed a wedding!" She sighed. "There's a lot of memories to buff out there."

Taj was impressed. "You guys work really hard to keep all this a secret."

"We have to," said F.T. "If people knew that their fun was being stolen by time thieves, they'd be too afraid to have any fun at all. And what kind of a world would that be?" Then he turned to Eon. "We should check the time levels."

Eon nodded and sat down at a sleek glass desk with a single monitor on top. F.T. looked over Eon's shoulder as he typed a series of commands into his keyboard. Then a grim look passed across both of their faces.

"What's wrong?" Taj asked. He couldn't see what was on the screen, but he had a feeling it was bad.

"Taj, remember when I told you that everyone was acting strangely today because they had too much time stolen from them?" said Eon.

Taj nodded.

Eon continued, "The forgetfulness, the exhaustion . . . those are all symptoms of Total Time Deprivation."

"It's a terrible condition," said F.T. "And it only gets worse. Dawn starts to feels like dusk. It's impossible to fall asleep at night or stay awake during the day. The past and present blend together into a state of confusion until finally . . ."

"Finally what?"

Eon and F.T. looked at each other like neither wanted to answer.

Finally F.T. said, "They become vegetables. Catatonic. Totally suspended in time."

"And at a certain point, it's irreversible," said Eon. He turned the monitor around and Taj saw a graph with a thick red line at the bottom. "This is the Timeline," Eon said. "If anyone's time levels dip below this line, we have a major problem."

"How long will that take?" Taj said, his voice shaking.

Eon pointed to a dot halfway down the graph. "The district is almost there. Based on my calculations"—his fingers flurried across his keyboard—"we have until noon tomorrow."

"Or what?"

"Or there'll be no turning it back."

"What?!" Taj shouted. "You're telling me that if we don't get the summers back before lunchtime tomorrow, everyone I know is going to have scrambled eggs for brains?!"

"In so many words . . . ," said F.T.

"Well, what about me? I feel fine and my summer was stolen, too!"

"We've checked your time levels," said Eon. "It looks like you're immune to TTD."

"A benefit of being the Worm, we presume," said F.T.

"Wow! Lucky me!" Taj scowled. "The lone survivor of the scrambled egg apocalypse!"

Suddenly, a loud blaring sound came from Ernie's station.

"Guys! Guys!" Ernie shouted, waving them over. "I think I've got something here! And it's not your grandma's teatime!"

Taj could see that there was a deep red patch on Ernie's screen. As he steered the joystick, the blaring got louder.

"That's the biggest concentration of stolen fun time I've ever seen!" said F.T.

"It must be the summers," Eon said.

"And they're on the move." Ernie yanked the joystick wildly from side to side, zipping the scanner through the city before zooming in on a building with a giant bowling pin on the roof.

Taj recognized it right away from after-school hangouts, weekend afternoons, and more birthday parties than he could count. "The summers are in the *Rock 'n' Bowl*?" he asked.

"Not *in* the Rock 'n' Bowl. Underneath it," said Ernie. "Time thieves have built a network of tunnels that run beneath the entire city. There's an entrance into that network at the Rock 'n' Bowl, and the summers are headed straight there."

"Let's go," said Eon. He turned to F.T. "We're going to need Special Ops."

F.T. raised an eyebrow. "I'm way ahead of you."

The door to the office burst open, startling Ernie so much that he screamed. The first thing Taj recognized was the headphones with the silver spiral. Standing in the doorway was Syd—the woman from the training facility. She walked up to Taj with a maniacal look in her eyes. She cracked her knuckles and grinned. "Hey, Wormie. You ready to go on a field trip?"

CHAPTER 7

3:14 P.M.

The bus screeched to a halt outside of the Rock 'n' Bowl. Taj watched Syd sift through a black duffel bag full of strange-looking weapons.

She pulled her headphones down around her neck and turned to him. "Always gotta be prepared," she said, strapping three silver grenades to her belt. "You never know when you're going to have to blow something up."

Eon held out his hand. "Toss me a Sizzler."

Syd threw him the same silver gun he'd used earlier

and he holstered it at his side.

Taj leaped to his feet. "Okay, so what's the plan?" he asked Eon. "You do the time freeze-y thing and we'll find the summers? If we move fast enough, we can probably get in a few games of bowling before dinner!"

"Wrong," said Eon. "As soon as we freeze time, the thieves will know we're there and they'll come after us. We need to keep a low profile. And one more thing." He opened a small plastic case and took out a contact lens. "Stick this in your eye."

"*What?*"

"This is a Vision Modifier. Everyone at the Agency has one." Eon stretched open his right eyelid and Taj could see a thin outline around his iris. "It'll allow you to see the time thieves."

Taj took the lens from Eon. "At least it's better than wearing those glasses you gave me at school. They made me look like my great-aunt Phyllis." He carefully placed the lens in his eye and blinked a few times until he could barely feel it at all. Then he asked, "What's this thing made of?"

"The glass is made from highly compressed time." He pointed to his watch. "Same as the surfaces of our timepieces."

"Do I get a timepiece?" Taj asked eagerly.

"No," said Eon. He looked at Syd. "You ready?"

"I got enough firepower on me to blast the time thieves into yesterday. But all I really need are these babies," she said, kissing her fists.

Taj groaned. "You guys get all these cool weapons and I just get a trip to the eye doctor?"

"Taj, these aren't toys. They're very dangerous—"

"Aw, let's give the kid a Sludge Can," Syd said, reaching into the duffel bag and pulling out a small blue canister with a plastic nozzle at the top.

"This looks like an asthma inhaler," said Taj.

"Be *very* careful with it," said Eon. Then he tapped his watch. "How long do we have, Ernie?"

Ernie's nasally voice came through in reply. "The

summers are approaching the bowling alley but they're moving fast. I'd say you have three minutes."

The Rock 'n' Bowl was always packed with people—and today was no exception. The place rumbled with the sounds of balls rolling down the lanes and the explosions of pins crashing together. There was a group of college guys on one lane chugging root beer and eating pizza. Next to them were the real professionals, the older guys who bowled with total focus as if there was nothing in the world more important than breaking their own best scores. The rest of the lanes were filled with families. Young kids flung the balls down the alleys and let the bumpers do the work. Taj spotted a toddler stealing a bag of Cheetos from his mom's purse. The little boy waddled off to eat somewhere in peace.

Taj looked around. "So how do we get to this underground time thief network that Ernie was talking about?"

Syd's eyes darted back and forth and her nose twitched. She looked like a jungle cat staking out its prey. "Snack bar," she said.

"It's that way, through the arcade," Taj said, pointing to the next room.

"All right, Taj. Stay close to me, and try not to attract any attention," Eon said.

As they passed the group of college guys, something caught Taj's eye—a time thief clinging to the TV above the lane with its eight hairy legs. As one of the guys picked up a bowling ball, Taj saw something truly terrible. The time thief stuck out its thin yellow tongue and attached it to the back of the guy's head, slurping up a few seconds of fun.

Without thinking, Taj screamed, "LOOK OUT!" He grabbed the nearest bowling ball and hurled it with all his strength. The time thief leaped out of the way and the ball hit the TV with full force, shattering the screen and sending sparks raining down. The guys leaped back, spilling soda everywhere. The people bowling next to them were so surprised they slipped on the lanes, sending bowling balls rolling in every direction. Terrified kids hid behind their parents' legs and shrieked. Even the pro bowlers missed a few pins. It was total chaos.

One of the college guys whirled around and threw his arms in the air. "Are you crazy, bro?!"

Eon shook his head at Taj. "You *had* to throw a bowling ball into a TV." He tapped the red button on the side of his watch. Time instantly froze.

Syd stared straight ahead, like she was listening for some far-off sound. A smile crept across her face. "Here they come."

A horde of angry time thieves poured out from behind the bowling pins. They lashed their tails, licked their lips, and headed straight for Taj, Syd, and Eon.

Eon grabbed Taj's arm and pulled him to the front counter, where a worker was frozen in the middle of handing a customer her change.

"Take cover and stay down!" Eon insisted.

Taj leaped over the counter, straight into a gigantic pile of dirty bowling shoes.

"Ugh! Worst hiding spot ever!" he grimaced, holding his nose. He stayed crouching down for as long as he could, but the smell of sweaty feet and cheap disinfectant soon became unbearable. He came up for air just in time to see Syd deliver a blow so hard into a time thief's head that her fist came out the other end. She grabbed two more thieves and stuffed them into the automatic ball returner. She picked up as many bowling balls as she could carry and heaved them at the time thieves, squashing them to pieces.

"Don't mess with Syd!" Taj exclaimed.

"Get down," Eon said through gritted teeth. He was standing on top of the counter, firing shots from his Sizzler in rapid succession. Blue nets flew in every direction like the spray from a deadly sprinkler. Taj watched him take at least thirty shots in a row and he didn't see a single one miss.

Soon, there was only one time thief left. Syd scooped

it up and rolled it down the lane. As it collided with the pins, Taj yelled, "Strike!"

Ernie's voice came in through Eon's watch. "Eon, you've got to get to the summers! You have ninety seconds before they're out of reach."

"Let's go!" Eon shouted, running into the arcade.

Taj followed, but when he reached the doorway he stopped dead in his tracks. The scene was even more terrifying than the bowling alley. The arcade was crawling with creatures Taj had never seen before. They looked like caterpillars, only they were the size of baseball bats. They had big red eyes and skin so pale you could almost see through it. They wriggled across the video games and wrapped themselves around the legs of the kids who were frozen in place.

"Whoa, whoa, whoa!" Taj said, backing away. "Are those time thieves, too?! No one told me there's more than one kind!"

"One?" Syd laughed. "There are over six hundred known species. They've each evolved to live off a different kind of fun time."

Eon pointed back to the bowling lanes. "Those thieves are Cheaters. They steal fun time when people are playing sports—like bowling."

"Or dodgeball," Taj said, thinking back to the school gym.

"Exactly." Eon blasted a blue net onto a time thief wriggling across the air hockey table. It splattered everywhere. "These guys are called Creeps."

Taj ducked behind Eon. "What kind of time do Creeps steal?"

"Anything with screens," said Eon.

"Here, Creepy Creepy . . . ," Syd said, leaping on top of a video game. She grabbed a Creep by its head and its tail and pulled it in half. Its guts spilled out like the world's grossest piñata.

"So you're telling me when I'm watching TV these guys are watching me?" Taj asked.

Eon nodded. "It's why all the good shows seem to end so fast."

Taj watched Eon and Syd fighting off the time thieves and shuddered. Every time he'd been lounging around Jen's basement, these guys were there, too. Just the thought of it gave him, well, the creeps.

Out of the corner of his eye, he noticed a cluster of Creeps poking out from the Whac-A-Mole game. They were making strange babbling noises, like they were speaking in an alien language.

Taj picked up the big rubber mallet on the side of the game. "Now *this* I know how to do!" he said, whacking as hard as he could. But the Creeps were too fast. He whacked frantically over and over again, but the Creeps ducked out of the way just in time.

"Step aside," Syd said. She grabbed one of the silver grenades from her belt, pulled the pin out, and dropped it into the hole. "You might want to duck," she said.

Just as Taj hit the ground, there was a flash of green light and the entire Whac-A-Mole game exploded into a million pieces.

"Fun game," Syd grunted.

Eon sprinted ahead to the snack bar. "How much time?" he said urgently into his watch.

"Twenty seconds," said Ernie, unable to hide the nervousness in his voice.

Eon shoved the large metal fryer aside, the base screeching across the floor like nails on a chalkboard. Carved into the ground was a dark, greasy opening about the size of a manhole. Eon took off his jacket and laid it aside. "This is my least favorite part of the job," he said.

"We're going in there?!" Taj said.

"It's the Access Point, the only way to get into the time thief network."

"Wait!" said Syd. She dropped down and put her ear to the ground. "Time Flies."

"When you're having fun. I know," said Taj.

"No. Time *Flies*," Syd said.

"They steal your snack time," Eon explained, gesturing to the people frozen at the counter mid-meal.

Taj heard a buzzing sound, like a lawn mower, coming from underground. "Wha—?"

"Watch out!" Eon shouted, crashing into Taj like a linebacker.

As they hit the floor a swarm of enormous flies flew out of the tunnel. Their bodies were so big they could have been mistaken for bowling balls. There were so many of them, they looked like a black cloud.

"Use the Sludge Can! It'll glue their wings to their bodies!" Eon said to Taj. "Just make sure to point it—"

"Yeah, yeah, I've used a can of whipped cream before!" Taj pulled the Sludge Can out of his pocket and pointed it up at the throng of flies. "Eat sludge, suckers!" He pushed down hard on the nozzle and a deluge of gray glue blasted out—all over his face. Blinded by the sludge, Taj stumbled backward. He knocked over the napkin stations and crashed into the glass case of giant pretzels, sending enormous salt sprinkles everywhere.

As Taj hacked up the glue that was fusing to his taste buds, Eon said dryly, "Next time, try pointing it *that* way."

"Yeah, thanks for the advice!" Taj shot back.

The oversized flies whirled around, dive-bombing into them and making it impossible to get to the tunnel.

Syd picked up a vat of unnaturally yellow nacho cheese. "Out of the way!" she shouted, sloshing the entire contents all over the flies. The gloop coated their wings and they crashed to the ground. Taj wiped the last of the sludge from his eyes and saw the pack of flies flopping around on the floor, struggling to move through the sticky coating.

He grinned. "Hey, did somebody order Cheese Flies?" He held up his hand for a high five, but Syd and Eon were already climbing into the hole in the floor. Taj took a deep breath and followed.

Stretching out in front of him was a long tunnel coated with a grimy mixture of grease and dirt. It was cold and damp and smelled like stale funnel cake. He felt like he was inside someone's runny nose.

"Ugh! Why would the time thieves want to live under a deep fryer?" Taj asked, running up to Eon.

"Where there's fried food, fun can't be far," said Eon.

Taj nodded. "Lucas would agree."

"The hive is up here," Syd said, shining her flashlight up ahead.

They reached a burrow carved into the side of the tunnel. It looked like someone—or something—had been living in there. It was dimly lit with old Christmas lights and filled with tattered pillows and an old mattress, but besides that, it was empty.

"We're too late," said Eon.

Syd cast the flashlight beam all around the hive. She cut open the mattress, but there was only stuffing inside. She threw it across the hive in frustration.

"The summers were just here! They can't have gotten far," Taj said.

"The tunnel breaks off in fifteen different directions. They could be anywhere," Eon said. "We'll get Ernie to trace them again with the scanners. Let's get out of here."

They ran back through the tunnel and climbed out into the snack bar. As they raced toward the front doors, Eon spoke into his watch. "Ernie, the summers are gone. We need a new read on their location."

Ernie replied, "It looks like the stolen time is heading north toward . . ." He trailed off.

"Toward what?" Eon said.

"Uh, we have a small problem over here. Something's wrong with the scanners."

"What do you mean?"

"I lost the signal! We've gone completely dark!"

Eon pushed open the door to the bowling alley and walked out into the sunlight just in time to see a black drone the size of a small helicopter plummet from the sky and land with an earsplitting crash on the sidewalk in front of them.

CHAPTER 8

4:11 P.M.

Taj stared at the smoldering hunk of metal on the ground. "Is that—"

"A scanner," said Eon.

"That's what I was afraid of," said Taj.

Syd walked over to inspect the drone. It was a large black disc with four small arms, each with a propeller attached. Beneath the disc was a high-tech camera covered in glowing red sensors. Syd carefully lifted it up by one of the arms. As soon as she touched the camera, the glass lens popped out and shattered on the ground and a handful of the red sensors fell off and rolled into the street.

"I'm going to go out on a limb here and say it's busted," Taj said. Then he saw something in the distance. "Look!"

Throughout the city, giant scanners fell from the sky like superheroes that had put on too much weight. One crashed on a car parked nearby. It smashed through the windshield and set off a blaring alarm. Another got tangled in a mess of power lines, spraying sparks all over the road.

Taj saw the smallest look of panic flash across Eon's face. This was definitely not good.

Eon held his watch up. "Ernie, what the hell is going on over there?"

"I don't know! I'm freaking out!" Ernie shouted. "All the scanners in the district are down! We're totally blind! Somebody must have hacked the system!"

Syd spoke into her own watch. "Well, whoever did it is making it rain scanners out here!"

Eon added, "And we've lost the only lead we had to the stolen summers. We're running out of time."

Skyler's voice piped in, and Taj could hear the *click-click-click* of her typing away furiously as she spoke. "I'm buffering memories all across the city and I've deployed Erasers to every crash site."

"You'd better send some to the bowling alley, too," Eon said, eyeing Taj. "We had a little mishap."

"Don't worry," said Skyler. "We'll contain this. You find a way to track down those summers."

Then a strange noise came through Eon's watch. It sounded like a cat about to puke. "What's that?" Eon asked.

"Uh, that's Ernie," said Skyler. "He's curled up in a ball on the floor having a panic attack. But don't worry, I'll take care of that, too."

Eon turned to Syd. "How are we going to trace the summers without any scanners?"

Syd punched her fist into her palm. "We need to get our hands on one of those time thieves and make it talk."

Taj shook his head in disbelief. "They . . . talk?"

"Oh, they talk all right," said Syd. "And when I get my hands on 'em, they'll sing."

"Maybe we can find one!" Taj said. He ran back inside the bowling alley, where everyone was still frozen in time.

"Taj, it's no use," Eon called after him. "We blasted every time thief from here to the snack bar."

As Syd and Eon caught up, Taj spotted a thin trail of Cheeto dust on the carpet. He followed it all the way to a side room that was used for birthday parties. He swung open the door and, sure enough, sitting alone under one of the tables was the toddler he had seen when he'd first walked in the Rock 'n' Bowl. The little boy was frozen, his fist full of Cheetos and his face covered in nuclear orange crumbs.

Perched on the table, staring down at the toddler, was a single Time Fly, its tongue hanging out of its mouth, ready to strike. It was waiting for time to restart so it could steal his snack time. Taj came up quietly, took out the Sludge Can, and, this time, pointed it in the right direction. The Time Fly dropped like a rock.

Syd picked up the Time Fly and squeezed its round body. "Where are the summers?" she growled.

The Time Fly's giant red eyes shifted back and forth nervously but it didn't respond.

Syd pinned it against the wall. "Start talking or I'm getting out a flyswatter!"

"Me don't know!" the Time Fly croaked. It was the strangest sound Taj had ever heard. Its voice almost sounded human, but it had a quality like it could really use a cough drop.

Eon got right in the Time Fly's face. "*Think. Carefully.*"

The fly squirmed but Syd's grip was too tight. Finally, it whispered, "Past . . . time."

"Past time? That doesn't make any sense," Eon said.

"Tell us where the summers are!" Syd shouted.

Just then, there was a flash of bright red light from the fly's left wing. Its eyes grew even wider and it grimaced. "Oh no!"

And with that, it exploded like a bomb had gone off inside it.

Time Fly guts and gray glue splattered everywhere. Syd leaped back in surprise then spit out what looked like a piece of Time Fly eye. Eon took a handkerchief out of his pocket and delicately wiped the guts off his forehead.

"Gross!" Taj screamed, wiping slime from his cheek. "I think it got up my nose!"

"Look at this," Syd said, holding up a piece of the Time Fly's wing. Embedded in the surface was a small piece of metal. It was shaped like a circle, with numbers along the inside edge. It looked like a tiny clock, except with no hands.

"I've never seen anything like that before," said Eon.

Syd examined it more closely. "The explosion came from the wing. This must have been the bomb. But what set it off?"

"Or who?" Eon asked.

"Excuse me! *I've* got a question!" Taj interrupted.

"That bug said the summers were 'past time.' What does that mean?"

"The little twerp wasn't making any sense," said Syd. "Time thieves steal the present. There's no way to steal the past."

Eon took the Time Fly's wing from Syd. "Come with me."

Taj and Syd followed Eon around the corner to a drab beige office building. A sign above the door said Tax Office. As they got closer, Taj noticed that under the knob was the same glass pad that was on every door at the Agency. He began to suspect that this wasn't a real tax office.

Eon swiped his watch and the door opened with a heavy click. He kicked some junk mail out of the way that was lying on the floor and flicked on the lights. Inside, Taj noticed that there were no file cabinets, no phones, no desks. Instead, there were shelves packed with Time Tracer gear, from weapons to first aid supplies.

"Where are we?" Taj asked.

"We call this place a Vault," said Eon. "It's a secure remote office where Time Tracers can go to stock up on ammo, analyze data, or do anything else we need when we're out in the field."

Syd added, "The Agency has them posted all over the world in places so boring that time thieves would never go inside. Insurance agencies, law firms, office supply stores . . ."

Eon headed for a computer in the back of the room. "I'm going to run a GIM," he said. He held the time thief's wing up to the screen. "There might be other time thieves with this kind of explosive. Maybe we can find a connection that'll lead us to the summers."

"What's a GIM?" said Taj.

"A Global Image Match," Eon replied. "All the surveillance data from the scanners is entered into the memory bank. The GIM will examine the footage for duplicates of the relevant image then transmit a compilation of results."

Taj turned to Syd. *"Huh?"*

"Eon's going to put a picture of the clock bomb thing into the computer box and see if any other time thieves have it," she explained.

"Gotcha," said Taj.

A few moments later, pictures of time thieves began to appear on the screen. Eon swiped through them rapidly. In every freeze-frame, the thieves were stealing time from an unsuspecting victim. The same type of tiny explosive device shaped like a handless clock was embedded in each creature's skin.

Taj recognized some of the thieves—Cheaters, a few Time Flies—but then a series of even more fantastic creatures flashed across the screen. "What's that?!" he asked, pointing to the monitor. "No, wait, what's *that*?!" he asked as the next image appeared. "No. Forget it. What's *that*?!"

"Stop!" Syd called out so loudly that Taj jumped. "Go back."

Eon swiped backward to an image of a community pool.

Syd tapped the screen, zooming in on a little girl on the edge of the diving board. Right behind her was a time thief bigger than any Taj had seen so far, at least four feet tall. Its body was shaped like an ant's—three giant bulbs stacked on top of each other. It had a big round head and rolls of fat under its chin. Its dry, cracked skin was the color of a sunburn. And it was wearing a grimy sweat-stained T-shirt that said I'm with Stupid, with an arrow pointing directly up. The clock-shaped bomb was implanted in the folds of its neck.

Syd looked at the picture so closely that her nose almost touched the screen. "That's Teddy."

Taj made a face that looked like he had just smelled a rotten egg. "And . . . *what* is Teddy?"

Syd explained, "A Weekend Guzzler. They'll suck up your weekend so fast you'll go from Saturday morning cartoons to Sunday dinner with your weird aunt before you even see Monday coming."

Taj knew the feeling all too well.

Syd continued, "Weekend Guzzlers are a highly

evolved species. They're obsessed with humans ... how they live, what they do for fun—"

"Right down to the ridiculous clothes they wear," Eon said, pointing to Teddy's shirt. He looked at Syd. "You know this joker?"

Syd nodded. "Yeah. His hive-mate, Bubbles, gives me a lot of valuable information. Bubbles is a pretty good friend, actually." She paused. "For a disgusting, oversized time-sucking bug."

"Can you get a location on Bubbles?" Eon asked.

Syd checked her watch. "Take me to the deli on Oak and Webster."

They rushed back to the bus. Eon jumped in the driver's seat. Syd plopped down behind him and threw on her headphones. Taj sat down and picked the remaining sludge out of his hair.

So we're going to a deli, he thought. He had no idea why. Maybe Bubbles lived under the deli. For all he knew, Bubbles *ran* the deli. He could only hope that whatever the reason, it would get them closer to finding the summers. As he stared out the window he thought about everyone he knew slowly losing all sense of time. Did Coach Fig ever wake up from his nap on the gym floor? Did Jen and Lucas make it through the school day? Was Zoe still demanding a bedtime story? Taj didn't want to think about what would happen if they didn't find the summers but it was impossible to think about anything else. Time was running out fast.

They hit a bump in the road and he was jolted back to reality. "You know what this bus could use? Some seat belts!" he said.

Eon didn't answer; he just pulled the sun visor down to protect his eyes from the glare. Taj noticed that there was a piece of paper taped to the back of the visor. It was a colorful crayon drawing of a big orange cat. The words *Lea, Age 5* were scrawled in the bottom corner.

"Who's Lea?" Taj asked.

"My daughter," Eon said without taking his eyes off the road.

"You have a daughter?! Huh, you seem like the type of guy who would just have, like, an aquarium filled with weird-looking fish . . . So what's Lea like?"

Eon slammed on the brakes and the bus ground to a halt. He quickly flipped the sun visor so the drawing was out of sight. "Mind your own business," he snapped at Taj.

They stepped off the bus in front of Larry's Deli, an unremarkable corner store with a blue awning. Stacks of newspapers and rows of magazines lined the outside wall.

"Let me guess," said Taj. "This isn't really a deli. It's a surveillance center that can find any time thief in the city!"

"No, it's a deli," Eon said. He opened the door and Taj saw that it was crammed with aisles of vacuum-packaged snacks, a glass-doored refrigerator full of almost expired milk, and a sandwich counter in the back.

Syd slid a pile of candy bars across the counter over to the cashier.

"Hey, Syd," said the scruffy guy at the register.

"Hey, Larry," said Syd, handing him a wad of bills.

Taj leaned over to Eon and whispered, "Now I get it! Larry is an undercover Time Tracer. And the candy bars aren't candy bars at all! They're high-tech tracking devices!"

"Nope, they're candy bars," said Eon as Syd unwrapped one and ate it in two bites. She pocketed the rest.

"Okay, wrong again," said Taj.

Syd looked at Larry. "Has there been a pickup yet?"

"Not for another hour. You're in luck," Larry replied.

Syd nodded and headed straight to the back of the deli. As Taj and Eon followed, Taj rubbed his hands together. "Oh! It's all becoming clear! *Behind* the deli is a top secret secure location where we'll get all of the info we need to find the time thief!"

Eon thought for a moment. "Yup."

Taj pumped his fist. "I knew it!"

But when Syd opened the back door, all Taj saw was

a dingy alley that was totally empty except for a giant dumpster.

Before Taj could ask what was happening, Syd swung open the dumpster lid and leaped inside. The smell of rancid food filled Taj's nose.

"Are you crazy?!" Taj shouted. "Get out of there!"

Syd banged around inside the metal dumpster, chucking out pieces of trash one by one. Taj ducked just in time to avoid a piece of old bologna with an eggshell stuck to it. Eon stood casually with his arms crossed, like this was all perfectly normal.

Then Taj heard Syd from deep inside the dumpster: "Jackpot!"

CHAPTER 9

4:40 P.M.

Syd climbed out of the dumpster holding an old newspaper with a piece of American cheese stuck to the pages. "Anyone want this?" she asked, peeling the cheese off and tossing it to Taj.

"Agh!" Taj shouted in disgust. "Syd, you know they have new newspapers at the *front* of the store."

"True, but not last Saturday's." She showed Taj the date at the top of the page. "Best way to find a Weekend Guzzler is to figure out the most fun thing that happened during the weekend." She began to flip through the different sections. "Come on . . . come on . . ."

Eon pointed to an advertisement. "Jazz in the park? That sounds fun."

"Wrong!" said Taj.

Syd nodded in agreement and kept looking.

"What about this lecture at the school of dentistry?" said Eon, tapping the bottom of the page.

Syd read the title. "'A History of Floss: A Long String of Events.'"

"Sounds informative," said Eon.

Taj shook his head. "Eon . . . have you ever actually *had* fun?"

"Of course I've had fun." Eon thought for a long moment. "I went mini golfing."

"Oh yeah? When?" asked Taj.

Eon's jaw clenched. "Twelve years ago."

Taj let out a long sigh. "Let me see that." He grabbed the paper and flipped all the way to the back. "Here!" he said. Amidst a smattering of colorful coupons was an advertisement for Union Square mall. In bright red block letters it said *BLOWOUT SALE! TWO DAYZ ONLY!* Taj's face lit up. "If there are words that end in a *Z*, you know it's got to be fun."

Syd pulled a piece of soggy bacon out of her hair, tossed it aside, and smiled. "Let's go shopping."

Taj, Eon, and Syd walked through the revolving doors onto the ground floor of Union Square mall. Shoppers strolled past the storefronts, their shoes tapping against the polished white floor.

Syd surveyed the scene. "If I know Bubbles, he's hanging around in a hive underneath the building." She walked forward briskly like she knew exactly where she was going. "There's an Access Point into the time thief network in the food court."

"How do you know?" asked Taj.

"I've spent a lot of time at this mall. Squashed a *ton* of time thieves here. Also, I bought a hat once at the Cowboy Supply Store. It wasn't a good look for me."

They wove through the crowd and darted around the kiosks until they reached the food court, where the lights were bright and the tables were full. It smelled like pizza and cheeseburgers baked together in one enormous cinnamon bun. Taj breathed in deep. "That's the smell of good times."

Eon gave Taj a warning look. "Stay focused."

"Okay, okay," said Taj.

"The Access Point is through there." Syd pointed to the Quick Koala, a Chinese food buffet that was famous for serving fifteen different chicken dishes. A burly man in a white paper hat heaped piles of chicken and noodles onto plate after plate as a line of customers shuffled past.

"We have to get behind the counter," said Eon.

Syd narrowed her eyes. "I'll puncture the fuel tank connected to the gas burners and fill the place with methane. Then everyone falls asleep and the path is clear."

Eon shook his head. "I'm going to have to veto that. We need a plan that *won't* potentially blow up the entire mall."

Syd shrugged. "Then I'm out of ideas."

"Follow my lead," said Eon. He marched up to the very front of the line, ignoring the angry protests from the customers.

"Can I help you?" said the man behind the counter.

"My name is Roger Q. Higgins. Health Department Inspector." Eon flipped his wallet open and closed so quickly that the man couldn't possibly read his ID. He continued loud enough for everyone to hear. "This establishment is under investigation for a mouse infestation."

The customers dropped their trays and hurried away in disgust.

Eon tried to go behind the counter, but the man blocked him, his arms crossed. "I didn't hear nothin' about a health inspection."

All at once, Syd grabbed the man by the collar and

growled, "If you don't get out of our way, I'll stuff you so full of chicken, you'll squawk."

Eon cleared his throat. "My—associate—is very passionate about food safety." He shot Syd a look and she reluctantly released her grip.

The man scowled then lifted up the barrier for Syd and Eon. But when Taj tried to follow, the man slammed it back down and said, "Who's he?"

"Junior Food Inspector," said Eon.

Taj grinned. "Who do you think inspects the baby carrots?"

The man eyed him suspiciously, but let him through.

Inside the kitchen, a cook wearing a hair net stood at a stove, sautéing meat and vegetables.

"Health Department," Eon said, brushing past her.

Syd pushed the deep fryer to the side. Sure enough, there was a large hole in the ground. But it was completely sealed shut with concrete and plaster.

"What happened?!" said Syd.

The cook put down her spatula. "You guys were

just here last week. Told us to plug up that giant mouse hole. Must've been a big mouse. Probably ate a lot of chicken," she said, shaking her head.

Syd kicked the fryer in frustration.

Back in the food court, Syd was fuming but Eon stayed levelheaded.

"This mall is a hotbed of fun time. I'm sure the time thieves have dug a new Access Point by now. We just have to find it," he said.

Taj saw Syd's ear wiggle ever so slightly. "I'm on it," she said. Then she took off at a full sprint.

When Taj and Eon caught up, they found her hiding behind a pillar.

"Wha—?" Taj panted.

"Shh!" said Syd. She jutted her thumb toward the other side of the pillar.

Taj craned his neck and saw a big marble fountain. Perched on the edge were some teenagers, chatting and staring at their phones. And behind them, sitting in the fountain water, was the most disgusting creature

Taj had ever seen. It was gray, slimy, and coated in warts. It looked like a slug—but it was as big as a bear. It was slurping up time from the backs of the teenagers' heads and looking very pleased with itself.

"That's a Slouch," Eon whispered. "It steals people's time when they're engaging in general social exchange with no physical activity."

Taj raised his eyebrow. "You mean just hanging out?"

"Sure," said Eon. "We can follow the Slouch to the Access Point but if it notices us, it'll attack."

"And you do *not* want to tangle with a Slouch," Syd added. "Those teeth are deadly."

Taj didn't see any teeth at all in the creature's mouth, just some soggy gums, but he still didn't want to take any chances.

"Only problem is, the Slouch won't leave until those kids do," said Syd.

Taj shook his head. "Then we'll be here all day. High schoolers would sleep at the mall if they could."

Eon went over to the information desk and said something to the woman in charge, but Taj couldn't hear what it was. Just as Eon got back, the woman made an announcement over the loudspeaker. "Attention teenagers sitting on the fountain. Your parents are here to take family portraits with you."

And with that, the teens sprang up, horrified. They looked at each other, not sure what to do, then all ran away in different directions.

"The Slouch is on the move!" Syd whispered.

But "on the move" was an exaggeration. The Slouch wriggled out of the fountain at a painstakingly slow pace. It crawled through the mall, leaving a trail of pale green mucous on the floor.

Syd, Taj, and Eon followed at a distance, one very small step at a time.

Taj let out a long, frustrated sigh. "This thing needs to pick up the pace! Eon, go give it a kick in the tail!"

"This job takes patience," said Eon.

"That's right," said Syd. "Let me tell you a story

about patience." She pulled a candy bar from her pocket and began peeling off the wrapper. "Two summers ago. Tokyo Olympics. The whole place was getting hammered by Travel Bugs."

"What are Travel Bugs?" Taj asked as he took another tiny step forward.

"They attack unsuspecting tourists when they're on vacation. And let me tell you, those little suckers are feisty. Forty thousand international spectators were about to lose all memory of how they got to Tokyo in the first place." She took a big bite of the candy bar. "I'd been tracking the biggest bug for days. Finally cornered it in an empty locker room. That's when things got hairy. Because Travel Bugs"—she leaned in close to Taj—"they've got a temper. It whipped its stinger out and nailed me here, here, and here," She pointed to a spot on her arm, her leg, and the middle of her eyeball. "And wouldn't you know it, I'm all out of antivenom! So I'm swelling up so big, I look like a balloon in the Thanksgiving Day Parade. I'm stumbling around, I can barely see. I thought I was done for. But then, as luck would have it, I crash into a closet where they're storing the javelins—you know, for the track and field? So I grab one and *WHA-PA!*" She made a motion like she was throwing a giant dart. "Pinned the little pest against the wall. It tried to wriggle free but I popped its head off with my bare hands. Just then, the Canadian track team walked in. I was about to freeze time when I realized my watch got totally busted in the fight! So I grabbed the dead bug and jumped into a locker. Long story short, I stayed in there for two days, living off whatever sweat I could squeeze out of the dirty socks. So, like I said . . . patience." She crammed the rest of the candy bar in her mouth and smiled. "I love the Olympics."

Taj's mouth hung open. "Is that how you got that scar?"

"Oh, this?" She pointed to the scar running down the left side of her face. "No. That's a *really* crazy story—"

"Stop!" Eon whispered, holding out his arms. "I think it heard us."

The giant Slouch lifted its head and ever so slowly twisted its neck to look behind it.

"Everybody play it cool!" Taj turned to the closest kiosk and grabbed a handful of accessories. He threw a pair of oversized sunglasses on Eon's face and wrapped his own head in a lacy scarf. Then he tossed Syd a cowboy hat.

She frowned. "I told you it's not my look."

"Just put it on!"

By the time the Slouch turned around, they looked like three regular shoppers admiring themselves in the mirror. The Slouch continued on its way. It slithered past a jewelry store then wove around a smoothie stand.

Just when Taj couldn't wait any longer, the Slouch changed course. It was heading straight for a big metal garbage can in front of a pet store.

"I know where the Access Point is!" Taj shouted.

"Taj, no—" Eon said, but Taj was already sprinting ahead.

Taj stuck his head inside the garbage can. The bottom had been torn out to make way for a hole in the ground.

"It's in here!" he shouted.

But when he pulled his head back up, he was face-to-face with the Slouch. It was staring right at him, drool dripping from its wide, pale lips. It reared up to its full height, towering over him. And that's when Taj saw the teeth. There were hundreds of them, razor-sharp, lining the Slouch's entire underbelly, just inches away from Taj's head. He screamed at the top of his lungs.

The Slouch bore down on him and just when he was about to be shredded to pieces—

Time froze all around him. He heard the CRACK! of Eon's Sizzler. A blue net squeezed the Slouch until it exploded, coating Taj from head to toe in greenish-yellow slime.

Taj staggered backward and caught his breath. He

stared wide-eyed at Eon. "Am I alive?"

Eon nodded.

"Am I covered in Slouch guts?"

Eon nodded again.

"Ugh!" Taj wiped some of the slime off his arm and noticed that mixed in with the guts was sand. A lot of it. "Is this—?"

"Stolen time," Eon said. "The Slouch was full of it."

Suddenly, a flash of heat rippled through Taj's body. He felt like he was being pulled in a million different directions. Then came the same sensations he'd felt when he returned time at the Agency—the hairs on the back of his neck prickling; the dizziness; the ringing in his ears.

All the sand that was stuck to his skin rose straight up above his head.

And just like before, he saw a series of crystal clear images, memories that weren't his. First, the teenagers hanging around the fountain. Then, people he'd never seen before—a couple lounging on a picnic blanket, a group of kids sitting by a pool . . . dozens and dozens of pictures flashed in front of him, like he was watching a bunch of different movies in extreme fast-forward.

When his vision returned, he looked up. The sand gathered above him like a storm cloud, then flew away in a straight line—not upward, like at the Agency, but backward—directly into the pet store.

Taj's jaw dropped. He turned to Eon, who had pretty much the same expression on his face. "What did I just do?"

Eon cleared his throat. "I, uh—think you just returned a bunch of stolen time to the people in that pet store."

Syd looked into the trash can. "If we don't restart time right away, the Guzzlers are going to realize we're here and this will all be for nothing."

"You're right." Eon pressed the red button on the side of his watch.

As soon as time unfroze, Taj heard a shriek from inside the pet store. A woman in a blue dress stumbled out with four parakeets clinging to her head, pulling her curly hair in different directions.

"Uh-oh . . . ," Taj said under his breath. "I don't think I returned the time to the people. I returned it to the pets."

A stampede of dogs burst through the door, barking and howling. A horde of fluffy white cats pounced out behind them.

Taj looked through the store window and saw colorful fish leaping from one aquarium to another. A Komodo dragon chased a little girl down the aisles. Lizards and geckos climbed up the walls. It was like all the animals had been given a fresh burst of life. Even the turtles scurried across the ground so fast that no one could catch them.

The frazzled pet store owner ran out of the store screaming, "The snakes are unlocking their own cages!"

Amidst the chaos, Syd climbed into the trash can and dropped down into the tunnel.

Eon grabbed Taj. "Let's go."

"But—do you see what I just did?! It's a disaster!"

"Taj, I understand you're worried, but if we don't get moving we're going to have a much bigger disaster on our hands," said Eon. Then he jumped into the tunnel.

Taj took one last horrified look at the scene and jumped in after him.

CHAPTER 10

5:04 P.M.

Taj landed on the soft ground. A dimly lit tunnel stretched out in front of him. Hives were carved out along both sides. Coming from up ahead, he heard a strange sound. It was muffled but unmistakable—*dance music.* Syd gestured for them to go toward it. As they walked they all had to stoop to keep from hitting their heads on the low ceiling. It smelled sweet and stale, like the tunnel below the Rock 'n' Bowl, but the hives down here weren't abandoned. As they snuck silently past, Taj saw that in each hive was a different type of time thief, and every hive was filled with piles and piles of sand.

Eon must have noticed Taj's confusion. He slowed down and sidled up to Taj to explain, "Under every city in the world is a network like this. Once the thieves steal the time, they bring it back to their hives to share with the others." Just then, a clump of greasy dirt dropped from the ceiling onto Eon's head. "I hate it down here," he growled.

Meanwhile, Syd led the way through the vast network like it was her second home.

A Cheater scurried out from one of the hives. As soon as it saw them, its eyes bulged in panic. In an instant, Eon grabbed his Sizzler and aimed. The Cheater shrieked at the top of its lungs and darted in the other direction, running as fast as its eight legs could carry it.

"Would you put that thing away?" said Syd, irritated. "I've worked for years to build up trust with these informants. You shoot one and they're all going to bolt—then we'll never figure out where those summers are headed."

"Fine," Eon said brusquely, holstering the Sizzler.

They reached the hive that was playing the music. An old door with broken hinges leaned up against the entrance. Syd pulled open the door just a crack and they peeked inside. Taj couldn't believe what he saw. There was a raucous party going on and every single guest was a Weekend Guzzler. There were dozens of them dancing around, giggling uncontrollably, their cheeks the color of ripe tomatoes.

The decor in the hive looked like it had been fished out of a wet dumpster. There was a dinged-up stereo with a hole in one of the speakers, and a couch made of discarded subway seats. Two Guzzlers played video games on a black-and-white TV with a cracked screen. In the corner, a few more jumped between two tattered mattresses like they were kids alone in a hotel room. And in the center of the hive was a mountain of sand.

Taj saw one of the Guzzlers grab a handful of the sand and stuff it in its mouth.

"What is it doing?" Taj whispered.

"Feeding," said Eon, his voice filled with disgust. "That's a pile of stolen weekends. The hive will live off it as long as they can. Then it's back up to the surface to steal some more."

Syd gripped the edge of the door. "All right, here we go. Taj, don't say anything. And Eon"—she gave him a warning look—"don't kill anything." Then she pushed the broken door out of the way and stepped into the hive.

"TRACERS!" a Guzzler shrieked, and the whole place plunged into pandemonium. The Guzzlers all screamed and ran in different directions, trying to stuff as much sand in their pockets as they could before stampeding out the doorway, down the tunnel, and out of sight.

But Syd didn't seem to care. There was only one Guzzler she was after and she had it cornered. Taj stepped into the hive to get a better look. He couldn't believe how enormously fat the Guzzler was. All it was wearing was a frayed denim vest that barely covered its belly. Its spindly arms were crossed in front of its bulbous chest. And even though Taj had never been so close to a creature like this before, he could tell it was really, really mad.

"Sorry, Bubbles. Didn't mean to bust up your party," said Syd.

"Well, ya DID!" said Bubbles. His voice was part shout, part buzz. Like he had a bunch of mosquitoes in his mouth.

"We just need some answers then we'll get out of your hair," said Syd. "Where's Teddy?"

Bubbles's eyes shifted uneasily. "I dunno any Teddy."

"Come on, Bubbles. I know you were hive-mates. I saw you together a million times. And now he's got a metal chip in him. Some kind of explosive device. Looks like a clock with no hands . . ."

Bubbles plopped down on the subway seat couch and pretended to busy himself with an old magazine, but it was clear he couldn't actually read it—he was holding it upside down. "I told ya, I dunno—"

"Listen, scumbag!" Eon exploded, pinning Bubbles down. "If you obstruct this investigation for one more second, I'll blast your guts into New Year's Eve!"

"Ah, cheese! Wazz this guy's problem?!" Bubbles blubbered.

"Eon, come on!" Syd said, pulling him off. "Relax!" She turned back to Bubbles, who was brushing his vest off indignantly. She pulled a jar of sand out of her pocket. "Help me out, and there's a long weekend in it for you."

Bubbles looked at it hungrily. "How long?"

"Thanksgiving," said Syd, waving the jar. "Four. Days."

"Okay, okay!" Bubbles took a deep breath. "Teddy went to work for some guy."

"A guy?" Eon said.

"Yeah, an ugly human guy—like you. A guy who's got his *own* swarm of time thieves. All different species. They've gotta wear that chip thing, but in exchange the guy leads them to *loads* of fun time—more fun time than any of us ever see'd! I guess they was goin' after some summer vacations. Sounded too good to be true ..."

"It's not too good to be true. It happened," said Syd.

Bubbles's inky eyes grew wide. "Really?"

"Really," Taj murmured.

"Anyhoos," Bubbles continued, "now the guy's taken over all kindsa hives through the whole city. Good real estate, too! Right under the funnest places." He shook his head. "It ain't fair if you ask me."

"He must be moving the summers through those hives! Where are they?" said Eon, rushing at Bubbles.

"I dunno! I dunno!" Bubbles flinched.

"A Fly told us the summers were 'past time.' Does that ring a bell?" asked Syd.

"Nope," said Bubbles. "That don't even make no sense."

"You sure that's all you know?" Syd waved the jar of

sand in front of him.

"I swear, Syd!"

"And if you find out anything else, you'll contact me?"

"Course! I'll juss crank the volume to eleven!" Bubbles said, pointing to the old, cracked stereo. Taj noticed that there was a device attached to the volume dial—a metal spiral that looked just like the silver spiral on Syd's headphones.

Taj looked to Syd, impressed.

"What?" She tapped her headphones and gave him a knowing smile. "You thought I was just listening to opera music this whole time?"

Just then, a Weekend Guzzler with a dingy red bow on her head waddled into the hive. Before anyone could say a word, she opened her mouth and barfed wet sand right onto Taj's shoes.

"UGH!" Taj jumped backward.

The Guzzler burped loudly then flopped over onto one of the broken mattresses.

"Taj, meet Turnip," said Syd.

"What just happened?!" Taj shouted.

"That's how time thieves transport the time," Eon explained. "They extract it while you're having fun and store it in a time sac, which is sort of like a second stomach. Then they regurgitate it."

"That's the nastiest thing I've ever heard in my life." Taj gulped.

"Bees do the same thing when they turn nectar into honey. You can look it up," said Syd. "And honey's *delicious*."

"Syd, can I get my long weekend now?" Bubbles pleaded.

"Almost," she said. "The man controlling the swarm—what's his name? What's he look like?"

Bubbles glanced out the doorway to make sure no one was listening in. "All's I knows is he calls hisself 'O'Clock.'"

Syd began to hand over the jar of sand.

"Wait!" said Eon. "So, this O'Clock guy promises

access to large quantities of fun time. And he's clearly making good on his promise, since he led the thieves to the summers. How does he find all that fun time?"

Bubbles looked at him blankly and shrugged all six of his arms at once.

But then Turnip sat up and said, "He's got one of those scanny thingies you Tracers love so much."

Eon narrowed his eyes. "How would he get a scanner?"

Turnip let out another long, thunderous belch. "He's one of you."

CHAPTER 11

5:22 P.M.

obody in the mall noticed Taj, Syd, and Eon crawling back out of the garbage can. Everyone was too busy chasing after the loose animals. Gerbils and ferrets scurried in every direction. An African parrot perched on a beam near the ceiling kept screeching, "Come and get me!" over and over again. Taj was pretty sure he saw a bunny riding up the escalator. He couldn't believe what a mess he'd made. But there was nothing he could do about it now. Eon was already rushing to the exit.

Taj caught up to him. "You should call Ernie! Maybe he can get some intel from O'Clock's scanner!"

"Absolutely not," Eon said. "If O'Clock is on the inside, he's watching everything. Intercepting communication. We can't trust anyone. Not even our own team."

"Not even Ernie?" said Taj. "He can't be a criminal mastermind. He wears Hawaiian shirts and sandals with socks!"

"Anybody could be a wolf in sheep's clothing," said Eon.

Taj shook his head. "Not even a sheep would wear that outfit."

Eon turned to Syd. "We have to go dark." He pressed a red button on the side of his watch until the face went black. Without hesitation, Syd did the same. Taj followed them out of the mall and onto the bus.

"If we can't talk to the team then we have to do this ourselves!" said Taj. "Let's get back underground and start searching the network!"

Eon started the engine. "There are thousands

of hives underneath the city. There's no way we'll be able to find the summers in time if we're just running around without a plan."

"We've got to try something!" Taj insisted.

Eon merged into traffic. "We have to talk to F.T. face-to-face. He'll know what to do. Every move we make, O'Clock . . . whoever he is . . . is going to be one step ahead," Eon said in a measured tone.

Taj felt frustration bubbling up inside of him. "How can you be so calm?! What about the summers? What about my friends and family? My whole town! They're running out of time—and we're running out of time to save them!"

"We have to be smart about this," said Eon.

"Smart?!" Taj threw his hands in the air. "You don't understand! You don't even know how it feels for someone you care about to have their time stolen!"

"YES, I DO!" Eon shouted, punching the steering wheel. He took a deep breath and put his fingers to his temples, like he suddenly had a massive headache.

"I'm staying out of this one," said Syd, putting her headphones on.

Taj didn't know what to say. A moment passed. He took a cautious step toward Eon. "Who was it?"

Eon stared at the road. Then he said quietly, "My daughter. Time thieves stole her childhood."

Taj was dumbfounded. "What? How?"

"Hoodlums took it. They're time thieves that steal childhoods from kids *and* from their parents. That's why adults are always saying, 'They grow up so fast.' One day Lea was in kindergarten, and the next thing I knew she was starting high school."

"They took a whole childhood all at once?"

"Not all at once. Not like your summers. They take the small stuff. Piggyback rides . . . Pillow forts . . . The little moments you don't take pictures of. But over time, those moments add up."

"But how did they get *you*?" Taj asked. "You're, like, the best Time Tracer ever!"

"When you have a family, you . . ." Eon bit his lip. "You let your guard down. But I'll never let that happen again—to her, to me, or to anyone else, if I can help it. I don't want anyone to experience that pain, that loss, like I did. The best thing for me to do is throw myself into this job and crush every time thief I can get my hands on. I've devoted my whole life to protecting people's time, and I couldn't even protect my own daughter." He looked back at Taj. "But I'm going to protect you."

Taj felt terrible for Eon. "So, you don't remember *anything* fun about her childhood?"

"Well, there was this one time . . ." Eon took a long, thoughtful pause. "Lea always loved animals. She was the most caring kid—the most caring person I've ever known. She was always begging me to go to the zoo or the aquarium, but this job is demanding. You don't exactly get a lot of time off. There's a park with a big pond not far from the Agency. One day, before work, I took her there to feed the ducks.

"So there we were, tossing out bread crumbs, when Lea turns to me and says, 'Dad! I wish *I* was a duck!' Then, before I knew what was going on, she jumped right into the pond. Started splashing around, quacking . . . It was the funniest thing I'd ever seen." Eon's eyes started to crinkle at the edges. "She's making all this commotion, and she shouts to me, '*You* can be a duck, too!' And I don't know what came over me, but I jumped right in with her. We were swimming around, quacking like lunatics! Everyone was staring. But I didn't care . . ." His voice trailed off and Taj realized that for the first time since he'd met him, Eon was smiling.

They got back to the Ferry Building and took the elevator down. This time, Taj held on for dear life.

When the door opened, they weren't on the ground floor but at the very top. They were so high up they were above the model solar system. Taj looked down on the sun. The Time Tracers going about their business below looked as small as crumbs.

"F.T.'s office is this way," said Eon, leading Taj down a long, curved hallway.

On the walls hung hundreds of pictures of stately looking men and women, all wearing the same gold pendulum-shaped pin as F.T.

"All the Father Times of history," said Eon, noticing Taj's stare.

"There's more than one?"

"Of course," said Eon. "This Agency has been around for thousands of years."

Eon pointed to an oil painting of a thin man with curly hair. "Preston Blair was a brilliant time scientist. He proved that a watched pot never boils." Then he pointed to a black-and-white photograph of a woman with a sharp nose. "And Elizabeth Clay was the first Tracer to successfully locate and trap a Creep." He stopped in front of a photograph of a man with a mane of thick black hair that went down to his shoulders and a neatly trimmed beard. His brown eyes were so light they almost looked golden. "This is Leo Wolfe. He was F.T.'s predecessor. A brilliant inventor. Until his time was cut short."

"What happened to him?" said Taj.

Syd shook her head. "A Snoozer. It's the most dangerous time thief out there, the only species we haven't figured out how to kill."

"What kind of time does a Snoozer steal?" Taj asked.

"Sleep time," said Eon. "If you ever feel exhausted when you wake up, you probably had a lot of fun dreams during the night that got stolen."

Taj shifted uneasily.

Eon continued, "Snoozers are rarely seen, but six years ago, we caught one. We kept it locked up here under the tightest security in the world. But somehow, it got out. Total chaos. It wreaked havoc on the Agency, stole top secret technology, and attacked Leo Wolfe, the man who'd kept it prisoner."

"It stole his time?" Taj asked.

"Worse. It killed him. He was a great leader." He looked pointedly at Taj. "And his greatest dream was to find the Worm."

Eon and Syd tapped their wrists in salute. Out of respect, Taj did the same.

Eon knocked on the glass door and from within, F.T. shouted, "Come in. It's open!"

Inside, Taj was surprised to step into a lush, fragrant greenhouse. The room was crowded with exotic plants and rows and rows of blooming flowers. A rainbow of colors stretched out in front of them like an army at attention. Graceful vines crept up the shining glass walls. The air was warm and damp, and it smelled of soil. A hummingbird whizzed past Taj's nose. The only sign that it was an office at all was a sleek glass desk in the corner with nothing on it except a computer.

Just when Taj thought they might be in the wrong place, F.T. popped out from behind a big pointy shrub. He was wearing thick, dirt-stained gloves and a canvas gardening smock, the pockets stuffed with metal tools—a spade, a trowel, and pruning clippers. "Taj! Eon! Syd! Welcome back!" he exclaimed. But then he saw their stricken faces. "Something's wrong?"

Eon explained everything the Guzzlers had told them.

As he listened, F.T. paced back and forth, rubbing his hands together. "This is bad, bad, bad," he said, his normally jovial voice racked with worry. "If O'Clock is inside this Agency, we have a big problem. You must protect yourself. From now on, only communicate with me directly."

"How?" asked Eon. "All of our communications are monitored."

"Not *all*," said F.T. He reached into his desk drawer and pulled out a gold pendulum-shaped pin identical to the one on his suit. He handed it to Eon. "Insert this into your watch and you'll be able to receive messages directly from me."

Eon fitted the gold circle into the back of his watch.

It fit perfectly.

F.T. held his own pin close to his mouth and said, "How now brown cow."

The text appeared on Eon's watch in bright red letters: *HOW NOW BROWN COW.*

"Good," said Eon, and his voice echoed through F.T.'s pin.

F.T. clasped his hands together. "Now, back to the task at hand. Before this Agency had any scanners, Tracers made detailed maps of the ever-growing time thief network below the city. Go to the archives and get those maps. You'll find the summers the old-fashioned way and then, Taj, you'll have your chance to return them."

"Hopefully not to the nearest pet store," Taj joked weakly, but no one laughed.

Eon pursed his lips. "That is a concern."

There was a charged silence.

"Taj, why don't you stay with me?" said F.T. "Eon. Syd. Go to the archives."

"We're on it like a bonnet, boss," said Syd.

And Taj was left alone with F.T.

"Come on, take a walk with me." F.T. led Taj along a weaving path of painted ceramic tiles that speckled the floor. "There are over four hundred kinds of plants, birds, and insects in here. I saw a chipmunk last week. Don't know how it got down here, but I do say my door is always open." He stopped and looked at Taj expectantly. "Tell me what happened."

Taj took a deep breath. "I returned time again, and it was a disaster! It didn't go to the right person—or even the right species!" He didn't want to say out loud the fear that had been running through his mind all day, but he had no choice. "What if we find the summers but I can't return them?!"

"Well, Taj, earlier today—"

"Earlier today I only returned a couple of grains of sand! Just a *few* seconds from a whole stolen birthday party! The rest just sat in my hand like I was supposed to build a sandcastle or something! And now everyone is expecting me to return the summers to my entire neighborhood?! That's millions of seconds to hundreds of people! I can't do it!"

"Yet," F.T. corrected him. Then he kept on walking.

"I'm not ready."

"Does a baby bird feel ready to fly? Does an octopus feel ready to hold eight different things at the same time? Life often gives you gifts before you're ready."

Taj looked down at his shoes. "I know you think I'm some all-powerful being. But I'm not that special."

Something shifted in F.T.'s eyes, like suddenly Taj was the only thing that mattered in the universe. "Oh, but you are special!" he said so proudly that Taj started to feel like Father Time really was, well, a father. "You have a remarkable gift, Taj. You understand that life should be enjoyed. You don't just have fun, you create it out of thin air! And not just for yourself, but for everyone around you. Do you know how rare that is? Why, it's more rare than this Kadupul flower!" he picked up an empty flowerpot.

"There's nothing in there," Taj said, confused.

"I know. It's so rare I couldn't get one. But if I ever do, it's going in this pot." He smiled. "What I'm saying is that I'm more likely to stumble across a whole garden of Kadupul flowers than to find someone like you. Think of it, Taj. You were able to make your little sister laugh in a hospital bed when your parents couldn't even bring themselves to smile anymore."

Taj's face flushed with embarrassment. "How did you—"

"I've had the great pleasure of spending the day learning everything there is to know about you. And now, I'm more convinced than ever that you are the Worm."

"But I'm telling you, I'm not good enough."

"*Yet*," F.T. said once again.

"Yet! Yet! Yet!" Taj said, getting frustrated. "I need to learn *now* so I can return the summers and put an end to this!"

F.T. let out a little laugh. "When you master the

ability to return time, the work doesn't end. It begins."
Then he spotted something on the ground and gasped.
"Crabgrass!" He got down on his knees at the base of a
large peach tree.

"What?" Taj asked.

"It's a terrible weed. It'll ruin my peaches! Just
one of these little devils can produce 150,000 seeds.
Can you imagine? My whole office would be crabgrass!" He took out his spade and started meticu-
lously digging around a patch of stiff grass. "Don't
worry, I've bested it before. All I have to do is carefully loosen the soil around the patch, and then pull
each blade up one by one. But I have to make sure
to get the *whole* blade, including the root, or the entire operation is a complete waste of—well, you know.
Care to join me?"

"Uh . . . I'm cool," Taj said. "You know you can get
peaches at the store, right?"

"Not a peach this delicious. Go ahead, try one."

Taj plucked a peach from a low-hanging branch

and took a bite. It was incredible. His taste buds did backflips and shouted for joy. It was even better than the time Lucas had created the Melty Supreme Cheesewich—which was two fresh-baked pizzas smashed together with mac-n-cheese in the middle.

"Whoa!" Taj shouted, sending peach juice flying.

"I told you!" F.T. yoinked out a single blade of grass near the tree trunk. "I'll be honest with you, there's nothing I dread more than picking crabgrass. But when I'm done, I get to eat these peaches. And it's not just the fruit. Every spring the tree blooms with pink flowers. Now, I don't eat those because, well, they taste terrible. But the hummingbirds love them. You see? Unexpected benefits in unpredictable places." He looked up at Taj. "Life isn't always fun, but every second is precious. Even the least fun moments have extraordinary value if you're willing to make something out of them. Imagine what you could do with your immense talent if you were willing to pick a little crabgrass."

Taj didn't know what to say. He wished that F.T. would just give him a simple set of instructions for returning time, but he could tell by now that those didn't exist. He finished the peach. All that was left was the pit.

"Keep that. It's yours to plant," said F.T. "The world could always use another peach tree."

As Taj put the peach pit in his pocket, the door to the office flew open.

"The maps are gone," said Eon, the color drained from his face.

"Gone? What do you mean gone?" said F.T.

"Raided. Cleared out. Like the candy aisle the day after Halloween," said Syd.

"This is very troubling," said F.T.

"That's the least of it," said Eon. He rushed over to the computer on F.T.'s desk and pulled up the graph of the time levels. Now the big red dot that represented Taj's district hovered only inches above the Timeline. "The time levels are plummeting," Eon said. "It's as if everyone had twice as much time stolen."

"How is that possible?" said F.T.

"Sleep time," said Eon. "Everyone's sleep time was stolen, too."

F.T. gasped. "A Snoozer!"

Syd took a deep breath. "I'm gonna need another candy bar."

"So . . . how long do we have?" Taj asked.

Eon's face tensed. "Midnight."

"Midnight?" Taj slumped to the floor. He felt like he was going to be sick. "Everyone I know . . . has until midnight?"

Eon paced around the room. "The Time Fly said that the summers are past time. And Bubbles said that O'Clock took over hives under all the most fun places in the city. . . ."

"Yeah," said Syd. "But a lot of good that does us. We don't know where the fun is. We've got no scanners. We've got no maps."

That's when Taj remembered that he had a map.

The Map of Awesomeness. The one he'd spent months working on, pinpointing all the most fun places in the city and describing them in as much detail as humanly possible. He just hoped it was enough. He jumped to his feet. "How fast can you get me to my house?"

CHAPTER 12

6:26 P.M.

When the bus turned onto Taj's street, the first thing he saw was his dad's boss, Mr. Diaz. He was still standing at the grill in his front yard, only now the flames coming off the barbecue were as tall as his roof—but he didn't seem to mind. He just jabbed his spatula at a burger that was charred to a crisp.

They passed the park, where some people were stretched out in bikinis, trying to get a tan in the chilly autumn evening while others were bundled up in winter coats and woolen hats trying to sled down a snow-less hill.

Across the street, a group of kids wearing costumes and carrying empty candy buckets wandered from door to door, shouting "Trick or treat!" A mailman slept on the sidewalk, his head resting on a sack of undelivered letters.

Taj spotted someone in the middle of the road. "Watch out!" he shouted. Eon swerved just in time. It was Alice from the ice-cream shop. She was holding a gallon of what appeared to be strawberry ice cream above her head. She shouted, "Free samples!" as it melted down her arms and left a pinkish trail behind her.

When they reached Taj's house, Eon pulled the bus over and Taj jumped out. He was about to run inside when he noticed a light on in Jen's bedroom across the street. Normally, by this time of night, she would be planted in front of the TV mashing the buttons on a video game controller, but now she was hunched over her cramped desk, banging her head against it over and over again.

Taj had to check on her. He ran across the street. Eon honked the horn and shouted, "What are you doing?"

"I'll only be a minute!" said Taj.

Jen's bedroom was on the first floor. Taj ran straight through her front yard and tapped on her window.

She slid it open and looked at him with wild, blood-shot eyes. "What?! Can't you see how busy I am?!"

Every inch of the bedroom was covered in stacks of textbooks and piles of paper. Discarded pencil stubs littered the floor, the erasers worn down to tiny pink nubs. "What are you *doing*?" he asked.

"You know my dad's rule. No TV until I finish all my homework," she said. She picked up a notebook and started writing furiously.

Taj looked more closely at the textbooks: advanced calculus, European history, chemistry. And it dawned on him. She was finishing *all* of her homework, right through to the end of high school.

"Jen, stop!" Taj pleaded.

"I don't have time for this," she said deliriously. Then she slammed the window shut in his face.

Taj turned around just in time to see Lucas sprinting down the block—*backward*. He was still in his gym clothes, panting heavily and glistening with sweat.

"Hey!" Taj shouted after him.

"Sorry, buddy, can't talk! Must run!" Lucas wheezed. "Gotta get my sprint time down!"

Taj ran up alongside him. "What are you talking about?"

"If I can get all the way back to the starting line, I'll be the fastest kid in class! Coach Fig's gonna be so proud!" he said then he pumped his legs even harder and disappeared into the darkness.

"LUCAS!" Taj called after him. But he was gone. Taj put his hands on his head. This was horrible. Eon honked the horn again. Taj knew he had to get to the map. But he was afraid of what he might see inside his own house.

He slowly opened the door. His mom was carrying a giant turkey over to the table. "Taj! You're just in time for Christmas dinner!"

His dad burst in through the back door, dragging a tree from the yard. He was completely covered in sawdust and sap. "I don't know what's wrong with this town! There's no Christmas trees for sale anywhere! I had to cut this one down myself!" He dropped the giant tree in the middle of the room. "Who's going to help me decorate?"

"I'll ... be right back," Taj said, backing away slowly. Then he turned and ran up the stairs.

He walked past Zoe's room and stopped in his tracks. The only thing he could see in the dim glow of her night-light was that her toys were all neatly in place, like no one had played with them all day. He flicked on the lights and there was Zoe, sitting on her bed, slowly pulling the cotton out of her favorite stuffed animal. Her expression was blank and her eyes were vacant.

He looked at the banana-shaped clock on her bedside table: 6:39. He knew that the town was plummeting toward the Timeline fast, but he couldn't just leave his little sister like this. "Hey, mini monster," he said, sitting on the edge of the bed. She blinked, but that was about all. It seemed like his sister wasn't even in the room, like she was a fake cardboard cutout of herself. Taj felt like he was back in the hospital with her, as if his worst nightmare was repeating itself. So he did the only thing he could think to do. He took a deep breath, crossed his eyes, and blew out his cheeks to make the absolute silliest hamster face of all time.

Nothing.

It was as if Zoe didn't see Taj at all.

He gripped her by the shoulders. "Zoe, listen to me. Hang on a little longer, okay? Everything is going to be all right. I promise." It was a promise Taj desperately hoped he could keep.

He ran to his bedroom and pulled out The Map of Awesomeness, with all its color coded intersecting lines and extensive notes along the edges. Even though he couldn't remember using it over the summer, maybe his hard work would pay off now.

"Past time . . . past time . . . ," he whispered. He *knew* those words sounded familiar. He traced his finger along the lines, over all the most fun places in the city. Extreme Lazer Tag . . . Indoor Skydiving . . . Hurly World . . . It could be anywhere! He pored over his handwritten notes. Then his finger stopped at the edge of the city at a place where he had spent some of the best afternoons of his life. Memories flooded his mind—roasted peanuts, the smell of fresh-cut grass, oversized wads of bubble gum. The pieces locked into place all at once. "PAST TIME! America's pastime!" he shouted.

He flew down the stairs, out the front door, and ran onto the bus. "We're going to the baseball game."

CHAPTER 13

7:10 P.M.

Under the glow of the bright lights, Taj, Eon, and Syd made their way through the crowded entrance of Giants stadium. Wind whipped fiercely around the brick columns but the chilly air didn't dampen the fans' spirits. The game was about to start and everyone was eager to grab their candy and popcorn and get to their seats before the first pitch.

"Last time I was here was during the World Series," said Syd. "The Access Point to the network is under a condiment stand outside Section"—she closed her eyes, remembering—"Section 108."

"Let's go directly there," said Eon. He pointed at Taj. "No distractions. No funny stuff." He sounded even more tense than usual.

Just then a round-faced man wearing a khaki vest tapped Eon on the shoulder. "Free bobble—?" he asked, but before he could even finish the question, Eon twisted the guy's arm behind his back and pinned him against the wall.

"What did you say?" Eon growled.

"You want two? T-take 'em," the guy stammered.

"Eon, chill!" Taj shouted. "He's just trying to give us a souvenir!"

Eon furrowed his brow. Slowly, he released his grip and straightened his suit. The guy backed away, then turned and ran, leaving a canvas bag of bobbleheads on the ground.

"Hey, tough guy!" Taj said to Eon. "You're going to get us kicked out before we can even get to the Access Point. This is a baseball game! People are here to enjoy themselves. *Re-lax!*"

"Fine," Eon said through gritted teeth.

Syd picked up a bobblehead and ripped the head clean off. Eon and Taj stared at her.

"Just practicing," she mumbled.

They made their way past merchandise shops with displays of autographed jerseys, miniature wooden bats, and huge foam fingers. Every few feet there was another snack counter, with lines of people waiting to be served. They darted around a man carrying a gallon-sized cup of soda.

Eon shook his head. "Who could ever drink that much soda?"

"Are you kidding?" said Taj. "That's a medium!"

They finally got to Section 108, which was right next to first base.

"This is where all the fly balls land," Taj said. "Probably why the time thieves set up camp here."

They approached the condiment stand, which was smattered with unnaturally colored sauce dispensers, plastic tubs filled with diced relish and onions, and about a million tiny paper cups.

Eon turned to Syd and Taj. "If the summers are down there, the time thieves aren't going to give them up without a fight. This could get ugly." He discreetly placed his hand on his Sizzler.

Syd cracked her knuckles. "Taj, you stay behind me." She balled up her hands. "Fists, you stay in front of me."

She gave Eon a nod and he pushed the condiment stand to the side. The tunnel was there. But it did *not* look like the ones Taj had seen at the bowling alley or the mall. It was completely clogged up with slimy yellow gunk.

"Uh . . ." Taj looked at Syd and Eon. "Did you guys bring Kleenex?"

"Dammit," Syd muttered. "They clogged it."

"What does that mean?" Taj asked.

"They're on lockdown," said Eon. "Nothing in, noth-ing out. Explains why we haven't seen any time thieves here yet. This place is usually crawling with them."

Taj realized that Eon was right. There were no Cheaters on the field. No Time Flies buzzing around the snacks. Not even any Creeps on the TVs broadcasting the game in the concourse.

"What are we going to do?" said Taj.

"This is a good sign," said Eon. "They wouldn't clog the Access Point unless they were protecting something very important. The summers must be here."

Taj was starting to panic. "But how are we going to get down there?"

Syd bent down and scooped up a fingerful of the yellow goo. She examined it closely. Then she smelled it. Then she stuck it in her mouth.

"*Oh my god!*" Taj screamed.

An elderly couple turned around in surprise.

"The ... mustard!" Taj stammered, trying to cover his tracks. "It's ... extra spicy today!"

The couple looked at him like he was insane but continued on their way.

"What are you doing?!" Taj whispered to Syd.

"My job," said Syd. Then she turned to Eon. "Crowd Surfers."

Eon thought for a second. "The only way to unclog the Access Point is to lure them out." He let out a long, slow exhale. "Crowd Surfers are fierce. They can steal time from a whole crowd in a matter of seconds. But they're greedy little suckers. If we can increase the amusement levels in the stadium, they won't be able to resist."

Taj looked to Syd.

"Crank up the fun," she translated. "All the way."

And for the first time all day, Taj felt like he had the skills he needed to take on the time thieves. "Eon," he said, smacking him on the back. "Let me handle this."

Taj ran over to where the seats began and looked out onto the field. It was the bottom of the second inning, and the score was still zero-zero. A drowsy, listless energy had settled over the stadium.

Syd and Eon joined him, and Taj saw that Syd was

stuffing her face with another candy bar. She had two more in her hand.

"Don't you ever get sick of those things?" Taj asked. "You know, they sell hot dogs here."

"Sugar's better," she said, tiny flecks of chocolate spraying out of her mouth. "Gotta store up energy in case we get trapped somewhere . . . like a septic tank."

"Has that ever happened to you?"

She narrowed her green eyes. "Twice."

Taj looked over to Eon, who just shrugged as if to say "it happens." "Anyway . . . ," Taj said. "What this game needs is something exciting—a home run, a double play, a steal. But unless Syd is secretly a Major League ballplayer, we can't make that happen."

Syd swallowed the last of the candy bar. "I did play softball in high school, but they made me quit after I stole all the bases. I still have them somewhere."

Just then, the mascot—a giant gray seal in a bright orange jersey and sunglasses—came onto the field. He clapped his hands above his head then did a halfhearted cartwheel. No one seemed to be paying attention.

"What's this guy doing? I've seen traffic cops with better dance moves," said Taj, shaking his head. "Being a mascot is the best job ever. All you have to do to get thousands of people to cheer for you is put on a costume and look ridiculous! Most kids want to be pro athletes. Not me. I've always wanted to be a pro mascot. I'd light this place up!" That's when it hit him. "You guys think you can get me down there?"

Syd and Eon stared at each other for the briefest moment, like they were talking without saying anything, and then they both nodded and smiled.

Eon handed Taj a five-dollar bill. "Go buy a large cotton candy."

"What?" Taj said. "Eon, we don't have time for a snack right now—"

"Just do it," said Eon.

Taj hustled over to the nearest concession stand and ordered a cotton candy.

The pimply teenager behind the counter swirled the cone around the machine, whirling up a puffy mountain of pink sugar. "Order up," he mumbled.

But as Taj reached out to grab the cotton candy, Eon intercepted it. "Young man, don't touch that!" he barked. Before Taj could object, Eon turned to the teen behind the counter. "Alfred F. Derringer. Concession Standards Management. You are engaged in a violation of the Concession Code, sections 103, 104, and 209."

"Huh?" the guy grunted.

Taj looked around for Syd but she was nowhere in sight.

Eon pressed forward. "Blatant false advertising. And I'm talking to all of you!" he said, pointing at all three concession workers behind the counter. Eon popped the cotton candy off the cone and rolled it into a ball between his palms. "This boy ordered a large cotton candy. A *large*! Come here. Look at this," he said. The three workers leaned forward.

That's when Taj spotted Syd, hanging upside down

from an overhead pipe just behind the employees. They were so fixated on Eon that they didn't notice that she was unclipping the badges from their shirt collars.

Eon held up the cotton candy, which he'd compressed into a pink, pill-sized ball. "Does this look like a large to you?"

The workers all shook their heads.

"That's what I thought! I'm taking this to Management." He pocketed the cotton candy and placed his hand on Taj's shoulder. "Come with me, young man. I may need your testimony." Then he turned on his heel and they marched off together.

As soon as they turned the corner, Syd was waiting for them, holding the three badges. "Anyone need access to the restricted area?" she said.

"Always!" Taj replied. He had to admit he was impressed.

They raced down a stairwell to the lowest level of the stadium. At the end of a long, white-walled hallway a security guard sat, half asleep, in a folding chair.

On the wall above him was a sign that said Restricted Area. Employee Access Only.

They showed the guard their badges and he waved them through. Taj heard Syd whisper to Eon, "I could have just put that guy in a sleeper hold. Would have saved us a lot of time."

The restricted area bustled with people. Ice-cream vendors restocked their trays. Camera operators whizzed by, wheeling carts full of equipment. A gate led to the bullpen where a relief pitcher was warming up. They were so close to the field that Taj could practically smell the fresh-cut grass.

They turned a corner and saw the guy who worked as the mascot chowing down on a meatball sub. His seal outfit hung on a hook behind him, next to the field entrance.

In a flash, Eon grabbed the mascot's suit and tossed it to Taj.

"Hey!" the guy shouted, stringy cheese dangling from his lip.

"Your lunch break's been extended," Syd said, sitting him back down.

Taj stepped into the fluffy gray legs and stuck the massive head onto his shoulders.

Eon looked at Taj. "Get out there and dance your butt off like the lives of everyone you know depend on it—because they do."

Then the announcer's booming voice echoed through the stadium. "And the fly ball is caught! Still no score! The top of the inning is over!"

Now or never.

CHAPTER 14

7:42 P.M.

Taj ran out onto the field.

"Here comes our lovable mascot, Lou Seal," said the announcer.

Corny organ music began to blare as Taj swiveled the head around to line up the mesh eyeholes. He saw people get up from their seats to leave—and those who stayed seated seemed to barely realize he was there.

He had to act fast.

He ran straight to the pitcher's mound and launched into the first dance move that came to his head—the worm. As he wriggled around on his belly, the crowd started to take notice. There's something about the sight of a person dressed as a seal break-dancing in the dirt that people just can't look away from.

"Looks like Lou bought himself an energy drink!" said the announcer.

Now that he had the crowd's attention, it was time for the Wave. Taj ran to first base and flung his hands high in the air. He jogged around the stadium, doing his best to hold the seal head straight and not trip over the hem of his long, floppy gray pants. As he pointed to each different section, fans rose to their feet and cheered at the top of their lungs. Taj felt like the conductor of a giant orchestra. He looked up at the stands to see if any time thieves had come out of hiding. But there was nothing yet.

He rounded home plate and saw Syd and Eon inside the entranceway to the field.

"Where are the time thieves? Everyone's having fun!" Taj shouted, clapping his hands above his head to keep the energy going.

"They need to have *more* fun," Eon urged.

Taj knew there was only one way to take it to the next level. "Get the T-shirt cannons!" He grabbed a microphone that was still in its stand from "The Star-Spangled Banner." Then he hustled back to the pitcher's mound and bellowed, "Who wants free stuff?!"

The crowd went absolutely wild just in time for Syd and Eon to wheel out three huge T-shirt cannons. Each one had a bright orange base the size of a lawn mower topped by a rotating chamber of T-shirt shooters. Taj grabbed hold of one of them and began launching shirts in every direction.

Taj looked back at Eon, who was singling people out in the crowd one by one, then firing the cannon at them with impeccable accuracy. He seemed to be targeting the people who needed T-shirts the most— like a little girl who'd spilled ice cream on herself, and the shirtless guy who'd painted *GO GIANTS* on his bulging belly.

Meanwhile, Syd spun her cannon around wildly, firing it like a machine gun and shrieking like a yodeling warrior.

Taj pointed his cannon up toward the highest rows. It was always the people in the seats near the field that got the free T-shirts, and now it was time to spread the wealth. "This one's for the cheap seats!" he said, firing off a last round.

Taj had the stadium in the palm of his hand. Everywhere he looked people were smiling, laughing, and pumping giant foam fingers in the air. The energy was electric. Being a mascot was even more fun than he had imagined.

But it wasn't enough. There were still no time thieves anywhere in sight.

And that's when Taj realized something. There was only so much fun the crowd could have while watching him. But if they were making the fun themselves, the possibilities were limitless. And all they needed were a few simple instructions.

He picked up the mic and shouted, "DANCE PAR-TY!"

Now everyone in the stadium was on their feet.

"All right, this dance has three moves: clap, slide, and wiggle around! Part one—clap!" He clapped twice and the audience repeated after him. "All right, that's the easy part. Now onto part two—slide!" He slid to the right and the audience followed along. "You guys are naturals! And now, part three, here's where it gets silly. Wiggle around!" He wiggled his whole body around, and everyone in the crowd wiggled like they had ants in their pants. Even Eon tried, even though it looked like his hips were made of rusty metal.

"From the top!" Taj said.

The stadium DJ got in the mood. He cut the organ and started playing some dance jams. The crowd worked themselves up into a frenzy of wiggling and giggling. Did they look ridiculous? Yes. But did they care? No.

"Now, play ball!" Taj shouted.

He, Eon, and Syd ran off the field as the players took their positions. But the audience kept on dancing. They were having too much fun to sit.

Standing on the mound, the pitcher looked absolutely befuddled. He was so distracted that when he threw out his first pitch, he lobbed it right down the center of the plate. The Giants batter turned on the pitch and connected with a *CRACK!* The ball flew over right field, past the stands, and out of the park.

"HOME RUN!" the announcer shouted.

The entire stadium exploded in celebration. Strangers hugged each other. Grown men cried with joy ... all while still wiggling around.

Eon pointed to Section 108. "They're here."

Crowd Surfers spilled in from the concourse. They had black wings with red dots, like a photonegative of a ladybug. A giant, evil ladybug. They fluttered above the cheering people, dive-bombing the roaring crowd to steal as much fun time as they could as quickly as possible.

Eon and Syd sprinted back through the white hallway and up the stairs toward the Access Point. Taj followed, but he couldn't help but feel guilty. The Crowd Surfers were feasting on a fun buffet that he had created. "What about all the time that's being stolen?" he asked.

"Believe me, I'd like to sizzle those thieves more than anything, but those people will be okay. Trust me, there's not a baseball game that goes by where people don't get some time stolen."

They reached the condiment station as the last of the Crowd Surfers soared up from underground. The tunnel was clear except for some yellow crust around the edges.

Taj grimaced. "I feel like a booger about to go in reverse."

They all leaped in and slid down the slimy passageway. When they landed, they discovered that Crowd Surfers weren't the only ones in the hive. Time thieves of all shapes and sizes swarmed them before they were even on their feet. Eon fired his Sizzler as quickly as he could but he barely made a dent in the thick cloud of Time Flies whizzing around them. Syd did her best to fight them all hand to hand, squashing a Time Fly here and a Cheater there but there were too many of them. The onslaught seemed to be never-ending. Taj flailed wildly as oversized bug bodies slammed into him from every angle.

"GUYS! A LITTLE HELP!" he shouted over the thunderous buzzing.

"Use the High Beam!" Eon yelled.

"Are you crazy? It'll short out the electricity in the entire stadium!" Syd shouted back.

"There's too many of them! We'll never make it through alive if we don't!"

A Cheater slammed into Taj's stomach and knocked him to the ground. He looked up and saw a Creep standing above him, its enormous eyes bulging. As it licked its lips hungrily, Taj screamed, "Whatever a High Beam is, use it NOW!"

Just as Taj was sure he was done for, a flash of light nearly blinded him. The time thieves seized up, stiff as planks, and dropped to the floor like they were on a Tilt-A-Whirl that had suddenly stopped spinning. The lightbulbs hanging from the ceiling exploded with a series of pops. And then—

Total darkness. Total silence.

Eon clicked on a small flashlight. Taj could see time thieves scattered across the ground, paralyzed but still breathing. Eon swept the sliver of light all the way across the hive, stopping when he spotted something slumped against the dirt wall. It was an enormous sack—big enough to hold a small car. It was made of a milky white material, just translucent enough to see what was inside. And what was inside was unmistakable.

Taj ran toward the sack, hopping over the time thieves in his path. He pressed his hands against it. He could feel the sand inside. Millions of stolen seconds—maybe billions! The summers were in there! Hurly

World, the 'Roni Games, it was all in there!

"That is one fat sack of summers!" said Syd.

Even Eon couldn't help but gawk. "That's the most time I've ever seen in my life."

"We did it! We—we actually did it!" Taj was so excited he was stumbling over his words. "I didn't think we were ever going to find them! I mean, you have to admit, it got dicey there, but then Syd with that High Beam—come on!" He pointed to the time thieves wriggling on the ground. "These guys didn't know what they were up against! Teamwork makes the dream work, am I right?! We got the summers! I can't—!"

SLAM!

Some unseen force threw Taj against a hard, dirt wall. He fell to the floor. His head rang with pain.

"Taj!" Eon shouted, rushing to his side. "Are you okay?"

"Wh—what was that?" Taj said, wincing as Eon checked the side of his head.

"No blood," Eon said, "but you'll have one heck of a

headache tomorrow."

"What was that? I didn't see anything attack me! It was like a shadow!"

"Over here, guys!" Syd called. She was outside the hive, halfway down the tunnel.

Eon pulled Taj to his feet and they ran toward her voice. When Eon pointed the flashlight ahead, they saw the summers being quickly hauled away.

Eon broke into a full sprint. Taj did his best to keep up even though it hurt to run. They whipped around a dark bend and up ahead they saw an opening, the end of the hive network—and the summers were heading straight for it.

Syd grabbed a grenade from her belt, pulled the pin out with her teeth, and chucked it as hard as she could down the tunnel. Just as it rolled past the summers, it exploded and the tunnel collapsed, sealing off the exit. "Nowhere to run now!" she shouted.

Whatever had taken the summers stopped in its tracks. It stepped out of the shadows into the glow of

Eon's flashlight and hissed, "I could say the same to you."

The creature was at least eight feet tall, with a spindly body and massive bowed arms and legs that ended in razor-sharp claws. It looked like a giant mantis, but its skin was the color of an oil spill—ink black and yet swirling with color where the light hit it. Its eyes were completely white, no pupils or irises.

Taj was so terrified he felt like he couldn't breathe. "What is that?" he whispered.

Eon clenched his fists. "A Snoozer."

CHAPTER 15

8:09 P.M.

The Snoozer took a step toward forward and planted itself firmly in front of the summers.

Taj whispered, "That's the thing that attacks while you're sleeping?"

Eon nodded. "Ever notice how when you hit the snooze button on your alarm, those ten extra minutes always seem to vanish?"

"Uh-huh," said Taj.

"Don't *ever* hit the snooze button," said Syd.

The Snoozer grinned, revealing a mouthful of gray

teeth. It let out a low laugh.

Eon threw the flashlight to Taj. "Stay back. And whatever you do, keep the light on him. Don't let him into the shadows." He grabbed for his Sizzler.

"I thought Snoozers couldn't be killed!" Taj said.

"That doesn't mean I can't try." Eon put his finger on the trigger but in a flash, the Snoozer leaped forward and knocked the weapon from his hand. It seized him by the throat, lifting him high off the ground so they were eye to eye, then threw him down the tunnel.

"Eon!" Taj shouted, turning the flashlight on him.

"Taj, no! The light!" Eon said, scrambling to get to his feet.

Taj swung the flashlight back to the Snoozer, but it was too late. The tunnel seemed to be growing longer and longer right before his eyes. Taj ran forward but the faster he ran, the farther he got from the summers. He felt completely disoriented.

"What's happening?!" Taj shouted.

"Snoozers can trick you the same way a dream can," Eon called out, "especially in the dark."

Syd cracked her knuckles. "That's why they're such a nightmare to fight."

Suddenly, the tunnel contracted again and the Snoozer appeared right behind them, its eyes glowing like headlights. In one quick motion, Syd snapped a handcuff around one of the Snoozer's rigid arms. But before she could get to the other arm, the Snoozer reared backward. Syd tried to kick it in the chest with her combat boot but it was too quick. It grabbed her ankle and flung her to the ground, knocking the wind out of her.

Eon pulled back his fist but before he could deliver a blow, the Snoozer blocked it. "Did you miss me?" it hissed.

Eon's eyes grew wide with recognition. But before he could respond, the Snoozer elbowed him in the face, cracking his nose.

Then it turned its white eyes on Taj. It leaned down

so close that Taj could smell its stale breath. "You're not a Tracer," it said. It sniffed the air twice. "You're the Worm."

Taj didn't have time to think. He stood up as tall as he could and blurted out, "Yeah . . . that's right! I'm the Worm! And you'd better step back because I'm really powerful!"

The Snoozer's mouth curled up into a sneer. "The summers and the Worm. Won't the boss be pleased with me."

"Huh?"

The Snoozer raised its arm. Taj was sure it was going smash him to a pulp. But it didn't. It brought its arm down and wrapped the other end of the handcuffs around Taj's wrist, chaining them together.

"*Huh?!*"

The Snoozer grabbed the summers and ran, dragging Taj along so quickly that he felt like his arm was going to pop out of its socket.

"Syd! Eon!" Taj yelled back, but it was too late.

The Snoozer crouched down and leaped up with immense strength. It burst through the roof of the tunnel, cracking the asphalt of the street above. It crawled out, carrying the sack of summers in one arm and dragging Taj along with the other.

The Snoozer pulled Taj away from the stadium, where the lights were still burned out and the crowd was flooding out in a panic.

"HELP! HELP!" Taj shouted.

But he knew he must have just looked like he'd completely lost his mind. No one could see the Snoozer, and so the louder he screamed, the harder people tried to ignore him. All he could do was try his best to keep from knocking anybody over.

The Snoozer turned up a hilly street lined with shops and restaurants. A cable car clanged down the middle of the road. Taj tried to grab on to a streetlamp but the Snoozer yanked him forward. He had no idea where this monster was taking him, but one thing was for sure—it wasn't slowing down.

Just then he heard a loud screech. He turned back and saw the bus speeding up the hill.

"Over here!" he yelled frantically, waving his free arm above his head.

The bus barreled through the intersection, sending the cars around it swerving in all different directions before it skidded to a stop at the end of the block.

But the Snoozer acted fast. It scooped Taj up in its cold, bony arm and leaped through the front window of a fancy Italian restaurant.

An explosion of glass rained down on the dining room. The patrons screamed and tried to scramble away, knocking over tables and running into waiters who spilled trays of food and stacks of dirty dishes. The manager, a squat, mustachioed man in a too-tight suit jacket and soup-stained shirt, gripped what little hair he had left on his head and screamed, "Young man! Just what do you think you're doing?!"

But Taj was too busy struggling with the Snoozer to even scream for help. He just wanted to slow the

Snoozer down long enough for Eon and Syd to catch up, but the more he dug in his heels, the angrier the Snoozer became. It yanked Taj around so easily that he felt like a rag doll.

"Watch out! Coming through!" Taj shouted as the Snoozer dragged him across a white linen tablecloth. He plowed through the bread stick baskets and sent an enormous bowl of spaghetti smashing to the floor. "I'll pay for that!" he promised over his shoulder as he careened off the table into the lap of a big-haired woman who was too shocked to get out of the way.

An extra-large sardine and sausage pizza that had been resting on a metal rack toppled over, landing on Taj's head. On any other day, he would have been happy to score a free slice, but today he had bigger worries. The Snoozer wrenched him forward just as he saw Syd and Eon stride in through the smashed window and freeze time in the restaurant.

The Snoozer turned to grin at them. "Come and get me," it hissed as it pulled Taj and the sack of summers into the kitchen. It was crowded with cooks paused at their cutting boards. A ten-gallon pot of stew bubbled above an enormous flickering burner. A butcher's knife was stopped mid-swing above a leg of lamb. The Snoozer tucked Taj close, using him as a human shield as Syd and Eon ran in behind them.

The Snoozer grabbed a knife right out of a chef's hand and hurled it straight at Syd's head. She snatched the lid off a pot and held it up like a shield just in time.

Eon picked up a heavy cast-iron pan from the stove and swung it at the Snoozer's head—but that's when the Snoozer flipped the light switch, and the entire kitchen went pitch-dark.

Taj felt like the ground had dropped out from underneath him. He was falling fast.

"What's happening?!" Taj shouted.

"It's a trick! A nightmare," said Eon. "He's in our heads! Tell yourself it's just a dream and you'll be okay."

"It's just a dream," Taj said, and as soon as he did, the ground appeared and he landed. Hard. And since he was handcuffed, he couldn't get his arms up to brace for the impact. He felt like a sack of potatoes that'd fallen off the back of a moving truck. Before he could even catch his breath, the Snoozer had pulled him out the back door and into an alley behind the restaurant.

The Snoozer latched onto the fire escape that snaked up the back of the building and started climbing. All Taj could do was follow, helplessly in tow. They quickly climbed up six stories to the roof.

On top of the building, the wind blew wildly around them. The Snoozer hoisted Taj over its shoulder and started to run full speed toward the edge of the building.

"What's the plan here, buddy?!" Taj shouted just before the Snoozer leaped off the roof without slowing down. He closed his eyes tight and screamed so hard his throat hurt, waiting for the big *splat*.

But instead, he felt a jolt.

They had landed on top of a passing trolley. Taj's eyes popped open and he gasped for air. He survived.

Somehow, he survived! But considering he was still chained to a Snoozer, he couldn't exactly count it as a win. The trolley rumbled farther and farther away from Syd and Eon, the only people who could save him.

The cable car barreled forward. The Snoozer struggled to keep its balance while gripping the summers in one claw and holding Taj hostage with the other. All the while, it looked straight ahead, its eyes fixated on a point far off in the distance.

A little girl on a street corner pointed at Taj and shouted, "Look! There's a boy on the trolley!"

Without looking up, the girl's mother replied, "Yes, sweetie, there's a *lot* of people on the trolley."

Taj was totally trapped. There was no escape. All he could do was hold on for dear life.

But as they trundled past Marina Boulevard, Taj heard a high-pitched screech. Metal scraping metal. He looked to the left. Sparks were shooting up the side of the cable car. Eon had pulled the bus right up against the trolley! Syd was perched on top, readying herself to jump.

"Syd, no!" Taj shouted. "You'll never make it!"

"Kid, I once jumped onto a moving bullet train. I got this."

Syd leaped just as the trolley broke left at an intersection. She barely covered the distance, grabbing the edge of the cable car with her fingertips and scrabbling her boots against the trolley's side to keep from falling to the street. It would have been an amazing rescue—if at the same moment, the Snoozer hadn't leaped off the trolley with Taj in tow.

Taj and the Snoozer landed on either side of the metal cable, suspended by the handcuff chain that held them together. It was like they were on a makeshift zipline. A shower of sparks rained down as they slid away, heading straight for the Golden Gate Bridge.

Eon tried to follow. Even from a distance, Taj could see the panic on his friend's face as he tried to separate the bus from the cable car. But that was the least of Taj's worries. The cable they rode followed the slope of a hill so steep they were nearly in free fall.

They hit the end of the line still going faster than the cars around them. They flipped over the end of the cable line and, for about the thirtieth time today, Taj was sure he was dead meat. But the Snoozer cushioned him as they crashed to the ground. The roar of traffic filled Taj's ears as a steady flow of cars whizzed across the bridge. Battered and exhausted, the Snoozer forced itself to its feet and hauled Taj and the stolen summers to the railing. The thin metal bar was the only thing between them and a sheer two hundred foot drop into the gray water churning below.

"You're gonna jump, aren't you?!" Taj said. At this point, he had no energy left to try to stop it.

"Shh . . . ," the Snoozer said. It looked into the distance like it was searching for something. Taj noticed the clock with no hands embedded in its neck.

But then out of the corner of his eye, Taj was

distracted by a flash of movement. It was the bus! Eon was driving it down the steep hill—in reverse! From a distance, it looked like little more than a blur, but Taj felt his hopes rise.

He heard the chopping of propellers and turned to see a giant black drone covered in red sensors—a scanner—descending from the sky as if the Snoozer had summoned it. The Snoozer crouched down, readying itself to jump.

Taj tried to buy himself some time. He grabbed the railing with his one free hand as the bus came to a screeching halt at the edge of the bridge.

"No!" Taj cried as the Snoozer leaped into the air. Syd burst out of the bus and pulled a blade from a holster at her ankle. Without hesitating, she threw it so hard it flew nearly fifty yards in less than a second. It sliced through the Snoozer's handcuffed arm, lopping it clean off at the shoulder. Taj fell back on the bridge, landing painfully on his wrist, which was still cuffed to the Snoozer's now dismembered arm. The Snoozer landed on top of the scanner, shrieking in pain, but still holding the summers tight. The scanner sped away, and within mere moments, the Snoozer and all the stolen summers were gone.

CHAPTER 16

8:51 P.M.

Taj was in shock as he stood on the edge of the Golden Gate Bridge handcuffed to a severed Snoozer arm.

Eon rushed over to him. "Are you okay?"

"The summers ... they're gone!" Taj cried.

Eon put his hand on Taj's shoulder. "We're just lucky you're still here."

Syd sifted through an enormous key ring with about fifty mismatched keys. "Hang on, kid. I know it's in here somewhere." She tried a thin copper key in the handcuff. It didn't budge. "Oh, right, this one's for bear traps . . ." She tried a tiny silver key and the handcuff snapped open. The Snoozer arm fell to the ground.

Taj rubbed his wrist. "Thanks. That was going to make raising my hand in class really awkward."

Syd headed over to Eon, who was staring out over the water like he was trying to crack some sort of code in the waves.

"Is it just me, or did that Snoozer look familiar?" Syd asked.

Eon nodded. "Too familiar. That's the Snoozer that escaped from the Agency. The one that killed Father Time . . . And the scanner it escaped on? It was stolen on that same day."

"The Snoozer had that bomb in its neck," said Taj. "The clock with no hands."

Eon whipped his head around, his nostrils flaring, angry as Taj had ever seen him. "Is it possible that O'Clock helped the Snoozer escape? That O'Clock is the reason that Father Time was killed?" He turned to Taj. "And now he wants you."

Eon pulled F.T.'s gold pin from his jacket pocket and inserted it into his watch. "F.T., are you there? We need a secure location."

Moments later, the watch beeped and two words appeared on the face in red letters: VAULT 84.

Eon drove faster than Taj had ever seen anyone drive out to a strip mall on the edge of the city. Between a florist and a barbecue restaurant was a small office. Written in gold letters on the door was Barton, Barton & Greene: Attorneys-at-Law. The blinds were shut tightly and the sign in the window was flipped to Closed. Taj could tell by the glass pad embedded in the door that this was the Vault.

Eon scanned his watch against the pad and unlocked the door. The inside looked just like the "tax office" they had visited earlier—stashes of weapons and a high-tech computer bay.

Eon shut the door behind them and peered out through the blinds. "All clear," he said.

Syd grabbed a giant weapon that looked like a rocket launcher and cocked it. "Don't worry. No one's getting through that door."

"So . . . what? We're just going to sit here and wait?" Taj asked.

"Until we receive further instructions from F.T., yes," said Eon.

"But—we've got to get back out there!" Taj said. "Am I the only one who cares about the summers? Am I the only one who cares that my family and all my friends are about to have their brains scrambled forever!?"

"Of course not—"

"Then what are we waiting for?!" Taj shouted.

"Quiet!" Eon said sharply. "If O'Clock gets his hands on you, we don't know what he could be capable of."

"I don't care! The longer we stay here, the farther away the summers get!" Taj took a step toward the door but Eon blocked him.

"Taj, I have to protect you!"

"Guys—" said Syd, but they weren't listening.

Taj tried to push past Eon. "I didn't ask for your protection! I'm not your kid!"

"Hey, guys!" Syd said, louder this time.

"Hold on!" said Eon then he turned back to Taj. *"What did you just say?"*

"I said I'm not your kid!" Taj exploded. "You can't keep me locked up in here just because you couldn't protect your daughter!"

Eon looked like he'd just been slapped in the face.

"HEY, GUYS!" Syd shouted. "Who turned this hourglass?!"

"What?" Eon spun around to face her.

She pointed to a shelf. Crammed between two Sizzlers was an hourglass. The sand was pouring down through the center, forming a small pile. "It's just been turned. Who did it?"

Eon and Taj looked at her blankly. Neither one of

them had turned the hourglass.

A look of panic flashed across Syd's eyes and at the top of her lungs she shouted, "BOREDOM BOMB!"

The hourglass exploded. Sand and sharp shards of glass shot through the air in all directions. Taj hit the ground, covering his face. Sand fell over him, coating him from head to toe. The paralyzing effects of the Boredom Bomb quickly took hold. Time slowed to a crawl. Each second passed like the world's dullest day. It was like being trapped in the middle seat of an airplane that wouldn't take off until you read an entire social studies textbook . . . like recess on a rainy day where the only activity was folding socks . . . like having to eat dinner with your parents at a fancy restaurant and just when you think it's finally over they decide to *order coffee*. Boredom in its purest form. Taj tried to move but he felt like he was slowly sinking in a prehistoric tar pit. He reached out to Eon and Syd, who lay in anguished boredom only a few feet away, but Taj was too bored to move.

As the dust settled, the door creaked open. A tall, thin man with long, graying hair and a scraggly beard strode inside. He stood over Taj and peered down at him, his brown eyes crackling like a campfire. He had papery skin and sharp cheekbones. Taj felt like he knew him, but he couldn't remember from where.

"So this is the Worm," he said in a gravelly voice. "It's about time."

Taj tried to yell for help, or say anything at all, but his tongue felt tied to an anvil.

"I've been searching for you my entire life. You have no idea how difficult it's been to track you down."

Eon let out a groan and forced himself to roll over. And as he looked up at the man, Taj saw his eyes fill with horror. He gasped out the words, "Father . . . Time."

And with that, Taj remembered. The hallway at the Agency. The portraits on the wall—the last Father Time. But hadn't he been killed by the Snoozer? Taj recalled the picture—his thick black hair, his golden eyes. He was older now, gaunter, grayer. But he was the same Father Time. He was the same man. He brushed back his long hair to reveal a gold pin on his collar. He spoke into it, "Hello, Eon." The words appeared in red letters on Eon's watch.

Suddenly, it all made sense. He had used the pin to trap them.

"You can call me O'Clock now," he said with delight. "Father Time didn't really suit. I've never been much of a family man."

Eon muttered slowly, "I thought . . . you were . . ."

"Dead?" O'Clock said, laughing. "Yes, what a tragedy. A Snoozer escaping the Universal Time Agency, murdering the fearless leader and stealing priceless technology. How could it happen? An escape like that . . . Some might even say it was impossible. Unless, of course, it had help." He grinned. "You see, I realized, if I wanted to live forever, first I had to convince the world that I had died. So I freed the Snoozer and took the scanner with me. I used it to detect huge quantities of fun time, which made it very easy to amass an army. But I was looking for the needle in the haystack. Someone generating so much fun, they had to be the Worm." He peered down at Taj. "And when I found you, I knew I had to have you. It wasn't easy." He strolled over to Syd. "Your bodyguard is tough, but not so smart." Syd looked like she wanted to rip his throat out but all she could do was squirm.

Eon dragged his arm around, trying desperately to tap the face of his watch. But before he could, O'Clock stomped on his wrist and the watch shattered.

"This is a private party. If you told F.T. about it, that babbling idiot would simply spoil my fun," O'Clock said, slipping the broken watch off Eon's arm and dangling it above him.

Taj wanted to jump up and knock this guy in the teeth but the boredom weighed down on him like he was swimming in wet cement.

"Don't worry, Taj. The bomb's effects will wear off . . . eventually," O'Clock said in a sickeningly soothing voice. Then he pulled out a bag and threw it over Taj's head. The last thing Taj heard was O'Clock saying, "We have a lot of work to do together" before the force of the boredom knocked him out cold.

CHAPTER 17

10:48 P.M.

When Taj woke up, he was alone on the concrete floor of a jail cell. The walls were coated with mildew and the barred door was browned with rust. There was a metal bed with no mattress and a toilet that hadn't been cleaned, maybe ever.

The boredom still slowed his thoughts like a fly caught in syrup. He felt like he had been mowing an endless lawn for months. It was nearly impossible to stand up, let alone try to escape. He had never felt so hopeless.

Syd and Eon were paralyzed back in the Vault.

His parents were stuck in a tailspin of lost time.

Jen and Lucas would never have any fun again.

And Zoe . . . well, he didn't even want to think about Zoe.

He was trapped like a character in a badly designed video game. But there was no reset button in here. There was no on-off switch. This felt like Game Over.

Taj looked around the cell, searching for anything to break through this boredom. He rolled onto his side and felt something in his pocket. He struggled to pull it out. It was Father Time's old peach pit. He felt the sticky, dried juice on his fingertips and couldn't help but remember what F.T. had told him.

Even the least fun moments have extraordinary value if you're willing to make something out of them.

Taj held the peach pit in front of his face and examined the dozens of lines and rivulets crisscrossing its surface. He focused as hard as he could on the unremarkable little seed, and he started to notice things he'd never seen before. It started to look like the surface of an alien planet or a miniature brain that had been dried out in the sun. He turned the peach pit over and noticed that one of the lumpy lines curved into a goofy smile, sort of like Coach Fig's face. Taj laughed to himself and realized, like a miracle, the boredom was gone.

He leaped to his feet and looked out the barred window in the back of the cell. He saw the black ocean stretching out in front of him and, beyond it, the San Francisco skyline, shimmering with golden lights. Right away, he knew where he was—Alcatraz, the long-abandoned prison. He had been going here on field trips every year since fourth grade.

From a distance, he could just make out the clock tower on top of the Ferry Building. It was 11:01 p.m. Time was running out.

"Wormie worm! You waked up!" Taj heard a familiar

voice behind him. He turned around and saw that it was Bubbles.

In the cell across from Taj a group of Weekend Guzzlers were bouncing on the mattress that Taj had seen at the hive. Turnip was there, and Taj thought he recognized their hive-mate, Teddy, by his I'm with Stupid T-shirt. They were all part of O'Clock's crew now. When Taj squinted, he could even glimpse a metal clock with no hands freshly implanted in Bubbles's neck. Their cell door was wide open and they were surrounded by piles of sand. Bubbles grabbed a handful and stuffed it in his mouth.

Taj's stomach dropped, fearing the worst. "Is that our summers?!" he shouted.

Bubbles laughed, drooling mud. "Nah. O'Clock don't give us none of that. Sez he's savin' it for hisself." He picked up another handful of sand. "But this ain't so bad. All you can eat!"

Taj pressed his face to the bars of the door and

saw that he was at the edge of a long cellblock. The rest of the cells were filled with different species of time thieves, feasting on stolen time. There was a cell full of Cheaters skittering up the rusted metal bars and bouncing off the floor, spitting and gurgling. In the next cell was a cluster of Creeps congregated in front of a small television set. They stared at the screen with glazed eyes, their yellow tongues hanging down to the ground.

Taj realized that his was the only door that was locked. The time thieves had free rein of the place and had made themselves at home. The Guzzlers' cell was filled with possessions from their hive—the broken mattress, the couch made of subway seats, even the old stereo with the silver spiral on the volume dial. And that gave Taj an idea.

"Hey, Bubbles!" Taj shouted.

Bubbles waddled out of the cell. "Watchu want, wormy worm?"

"Where's the party?!"

"*Huhh?*" Bubbles sneered.

"I thought you Guzzlers knew how to have fun. I didn't realize you'd been sucking up weekends at the library!" Taj jeered.

Bubbles was appalled. "LI-BARY! I HATES THE LI-BARY!" He grabbed two fistfuls of sand, threw them in the air, and caught them in his giant gullet. "Quiet! Reading! Wordz wordz wordz!"

"Then let's get the party started, man!" said Taj.

"Nah, we can't do none of that." Bubbles held up a plump finger. "The boss always sez not to waste our precious time."

Just then a large black Cheater skittered in front of Taj's cell. Taj kicked it in its round stomach and it rolled over to Bubbles. "Come on. How about some beach volleyball?"

Bubbles caught the Cheater and the corners of his mouth turned up into a grin. He couldn't resist.

He threw the Cheater in the air and shouted, "BEEGE PARTY!"

The Guzzlers bopped the Cheater around their sandy cell. The rest of the Cheaters skittered out to get in on the fun. One by one, the Guzzlers picked them up and tossed them around, giggling and clapping.

"See, wormy?!" Bubbles called out. "We knows wazzup!"

Taj shrugged. "I guess. But . . . it's still missing something."

"Wat?" Bubbles asked.

"*Music*," said Taj.

Bubbles's eyes grew wide like Taj had just come up with the best idea in the world. "Ah, cheese! You so right!" He darted over to the stereo and turned it on.

"Crank it up!" Taj yelled at the top of his lungs.

As Bubbles turned the volume dial all the way to eleven, Taj hoped with all he had that Syd could hear him through her headphones.

"HEY, ALCATRAZ!" he yelled, hopping up on the bars like a monkey in a cage. "Are you having fun tonight?!"

There was a huge cheer from all the time thieves. They jumped, they danced, they slammed into each other with sheer joy. A horde of Crowd Surfers flew out of their cell and slid down the mounds of stolen time like they were sledding. Turnip and Teddy built a sandcastle with stolen time. But as soon as they finished, they ate the whole thing. Teddy patted his bulging belly, and Turnip let out a powerful belch. Just as she was about to dive back in for more, the implant on her neck glowed red and she exploded like a tomato in the microwave.

O'Clock's voice rattled throughout the cellblock. "SHUT! UP!"

The time thieves scattered in terror. Bubbles unplugged the stereo and ducked for cover.

O'Clock walked slowly down the hall, holding a small metal detonator high in the air.

"Let that be a lesson to all of you," he sneered. "You are despicable! I bring you out from underground! I let you live in this palace. I use my scanner to lead you to all the time you could ever need! I give, and I give, and I give, and *this* is how you repay me?!" he spat. "*Wasting* precious time, just like the humans." He shook his head. "Disgusting." He scooped a handful of slimy Turnip guts off the wall. "Interrupt my work again, and next time, I won't be so kind."

Then he turned and looked right at Taj. His expression softened. "I'm glad to see you're feeling better. We'll begin soon. I'm just putting the final touches on my newest invention." He clasped his hands together. "And I am *very* eager to show it to you."

Taj's stomach soured like spoiled milk. "What do you want from me?"

"You don't want me to ruin the surprise, do you? Suffice it to say, we're going to have the time of our lives." He turned to leave then looked back. "Oh, and Taj? I know you've been dying to get your summer back. Don't worry, I set it aside. It's all yours . . . *if* you behave."

He strode into the Guzzlers' cell. Bubbles and the others cowered in the corner. O'Clock delivered one swift kick to the old stereo, smashing it to pieces. He walked back through the hall and out of sight.

Taj rattled the bars in desperation. There was no way out. He slumped onto the cot and put his head in his hands.

CHAPTER 18

11:31 P.M.

Taj looked out the cell window at the clock tower across the water. As the minutes ticked by he thought of all the times he'd stared at the clock in class, longing for it to move faster. Now all he wanted was for time to slow down. Anything to keep the clock from striking midnight.

He heard a key in the cell door behind him. O'Clock had come for him. Taj gripped on to the barred window. "You're not going to take me without a fight."

"Do me a favor, save it for the bad guy."

Taj whipped around and saw Syd standing on the other side of the door.

"You made it!" Taj said, rushing over to her.

Syd tapped on her headphones. "Got your message. Sounded like a fun party. Sorry I missed it." She sorted through her giant key ring and tried a rusty gold key in the door. "I stole this one from a Russian prison guard." She turned it and the lock clicked open. "Bingo," she said.

"Where's Eon?" Taj asked.

"Still making his way through the hole I sawed in the ceiling."

Eon dropped to the floor, a black duffel bag on his shoulder. "I'm getting too old for this," he winced. "Let's go."

But Teddy had already spotted them. His eyes bulged as he shouted, "TRACERS!"

"Looks like we're going to have to do this the hard way," said Eon as he unzipped his duffel bag. Sizzlers and Sludge Cans spilled out. It was like he'd cleaned out the entire Vault. He picked up a Sizzler and tossed another to Taj. "You ready?"

"As I'll ever be," said Taj.

"Just try not to shoot yourself in the face," said Syd.

"Got it," said Taj.

Eon, Syd, and Taj sprang out of the cell, Sizzlers at the ready.

CRACK! CRACK! CRACK! Eon blasted at time thieves one after another. There were hundreds of them massed in the old abandoned prison, blocking the Tracers' way out, ready for a fight.

Taj pointed the sight of his Sizzler right in the center of a Cheater's body. He took a deep breath and pulled the trigger. The Cheater writhed in the searing blue net until all that was left inside was a pile of sand and guts.

"Score!!!" Taj cheered. "Time thieves: zero. Taj: one million!"

"Focus, Taj! Focus," Eon shouted.

"Sorry!" Taj fired his Sizzler again and again, popping Cheaters left and right until he was out of ammo. He scrambled back to the duffel bag to reload, but just then a swarm of Time Flies flew into the cell and dive-bombed him. They slammed into his head and pummeled him with their wings. He dug through the gear until he found a Sludge Can. He pointed it upward and let it spray. Sticky gray glue wrapped up their wings and the oversized flies splattered to the ground like massive raindrops.

Taj sprang back into action as Syd passed the cell door. She was taking on a horde of Crowd Surfers, ripping off their spotted black wings one by one. They tried to scurry away but they were much slower on the ground than they were in the air. She stomped around and squished them with her boots like she was the leader of a demented marching band.

Eon cornered the Creeps in their own cell. "Anyone ever tell you guys you should cut the cord?" he said, unplugging the TV.

The Creeps' enormous eyes bugged out of their sockets. "Please! Five more minutes!" they wailed in a high-pitched chorus.

Eon swung the TV above his head, holding it by the cord, then flung it at the Creeps, smashing them into oblivion.

Now the only time thieves left were the Weekend Guzzlers, who were planted in front of the exit. But as Syd, Eon, and Taj moved toward them, they retreated back into their cell and locked it.

Syd laughed. "I didn't realize Guzzlers were such cowards." She approached the barred door and stared directly at Bubbles. "We had a good thing going, Bubbles. Why'd you ruin it?"

"Sorry, Syd. O'Clock gave me more time than youz ever could." Taj could already see Bubbles trying to weasel his way out of this mess. "But, uh, maybe weez can work something out?" Bubbles said.

"I have a rule. I only get stabbed in the back once." She grabbed a grenade from her belt, pulled the pin, and tossed it into the cell. "Time to pop, Bubbles."

Bubbles grimaced. "Ah, cheese. Dis is gonna hurt."

There was a bright flash of green light, then a massive explosion. Muddy Guzzler guts sprayed across the room.

Taj took one last look at the cellblock. It was totally trashed with the shredded remnants of time thieves. "Wouldn't want to be the janitor in this place."

They crept out of the cellblock doors into a long, concrete hallway.

"Come on," said Taj. "The summers can't be far." He turned a corner and saw the vast maze of Alcatraz stretching out in front of him. "Or ... maybe they can." The prison was enormous, an endless puzzle of twists and turns and unmarked doors.

"We have to move fast," said Eon.

They snuck down one of the corridors, Sizzlers drawn. They peeked into every dark, dingy room and behind every barred door, but the place was deserted. They made their way through the mess hall, where the paint was peeling off the floor and the stale rot of decades-old bologna sandwiches still hung in the air. They passed through the infirmary, a narrow room with a few old cots covered in moth-eaten sheets. Taj shivered. "This place gives me the creeps."

"Creep? Where?" Eon said, aiming his Sizzler in front of him.

Suddenly, they heard footsteps. Syd threw Eon and Taj against the wall and put her finger to her lips. Her eyes darted back and forth and her nose twitched.

"Travel Bug," she said under her breath. And at that moment, a huge scorpion-like creature skittered through the doorway. Its curved tail ended in a stinger that looked like a rusty needle.

Taj opened his mouth to scream but Eon covered it with his hand.

Syd leaped out and before the Travel Bug could attack, she popped off its tail and jammed the stinger into the back of its own head. It let out a tortured wail and exploded into sand.

She cracked her knuckles and smiled. "That was a fun one."

Eon frowned. "I thought we got all of them. Where did it come from?"

Then Taj saw something that made his heart sink. "Look," he said, pointing out the infirmary window.

Across the prison yard were more cellblocks, dozens of them, each filled with thieves devouring stolen time.

"Oh my god," said Eon so softly that Taj could barely hear it.

Syd shook her head. "The summers could be in any one of those blocks. We don't have enough ammo to take on all of them." She kicked the wall in frustration. "*And* I'm out of candy bars!"

Taj held up his hand. "Wait. Bubbles said O'Clock was keeping the summers for himself." Then he realized something. "And he called him 'the boss.'"

They sprinted up a flight of stairs and hid in a doorway at one end of a long corridor. At the other end was a door that said Warden's Office. Standing guard in front of it was the Snoozer that had tried to snatch Taj. Its white eyes stared straight ahead. Its shoulder was red and raw where its arm had been severed. With its remaining claw, it scratched at the clock with no hands embedded in its neck.

"What are we going to do?" Taj whispered. "And don't say fight it. The last time we tried that, it did *not* turn out well. I've still got pizza sauce in my ears."

"He's right. We can't fight it," said Eon.

"Only one thing to do." Syd yawned. "Take a nap."

"What? We can't just give up!" said Taj.

"Who said anything about giving up?" said Syd.

Eon shook his head. "It's too risky."

"I'll be all right," said Syd. "We've got to lure it away somehow."

"But . . . how?" said Taj.

"Kid, you have no idea how fun my dreams are." She turned and headed down the stairs. "Watch and learn."

Taj and Eon huddled close together in the doorway,

keeping an eye on the Snoozer, careful not to make a sound. As they waited, Taj realized that now was his chance to say something he'd wanted to say since he woke up in the jail cell.

"Eon," he whispered. "I'm sorry."

Eon furrowed his brow. "For what?"

"For what I said back in the Vault. About your daughter. I know I said I didn't ask for your protection. But let's be honest, I would have been dead ten times today if it wasn't for you." Taj's face flushed. "Anyway . . . thanks."

Eon was quiet for a moment and then he said, "No, Taj . . . thank you."

"Me?"

Eon nodded. "I've always fought to protect other people's fun time. But I didn't realize that I've been afraid to have any fun myself. I guess I was worried it would just . . . get stolen again. Today you reminded me what a fun place the world can be."

Taj grinned. "Firing that T-shirt cannon was pretty awesome, right?"

"Coolest thing I've ever done."

Just then they saw the Snoozer swivel its head from side to side and sniff the air. Its lip twitched. Taj could tell it was getting agitated—it was acting a lot like Lucas did ten minutes before lunchtime. Without warning, it pounced forward. Taj and Eon held their breath as it galloped past the doorway and bounded down the stairs.

The coast was clear.

Eon and Taj quietly made their way to the warden's office.

Eon steeled his face, pointed the Sizzler in front of him, and kicked open the door.

The first thing Taj spotted was the summers, still in the sack. They were in the center of the large office. On the warden's desk was O'Clock's metal detonator and a row of computer screens. O'Clock's back was to them. He was staring intently at a clock on the wall with no hands.

"Freeze, dirtbag," said Eon. "Any sudden movements and I deep-fry your brain."

O'Clock didn't move—not even to turn around to face them. "Never underestimate Eon. You always were my best Tracer. So noble. So serious."

"Enough." Eon took a few steps forward until the Sizzler was just inches away from the back of O'Clock's head. He nodded at Taj. "Go."

Taj ran to the summers.

O'Clock spun around to knock the Sizzler out of Eon's hand. But just as quickly, Eon seized him by the neck, lifted him up off the ground, and pinned him against the wall.

O'Clock squirmed, a vein bulging in his forehead. "Can't blame me for trying," he gurgled.

Taj grabbed an old letter opener from the warden's desk and stabbed it into the sack, tearing it open. The stolen summers spilled out onto the floor.

"No!" O'Clock cried.

Now was Taj's chance. He fell to the floor, closed his eyes, and shoved his hands into the sand.

He felt the familiar surge of heat. The flash of images. An ice-cream sample. A water balloon. The crack of a bat. He opened his eyes and saw a few grains shooting up toward the sky. But that was it.

He grasped for more, digging his hands in desperately. Nothing happened.

O'Clock choked out a laugh.

Taj focused every ounce of his being into returning the time. But it wasn't enough. "Eon," he said quietly. "I can't do it."

Eon turned to Taj, just for a moment. But it was a moment too long. O'Clock reached into his jacket. He pulled out the minute hand that was missing from the clock on the wall and plunged it into Eon's heart.

"NO!" Taj yelled.

Eon opened his mouth to scream but no sound came out. O'Clock twisted the blade in his chest, then pulled it out and tossed it aside. "I knew that one day this job would kill you."

Eon let out one last gasp and fell to the floor.

O'Clock picked up Eon's Sizzler and trained it on Taj. "Enough wasting time. Now the real fun can get started!"

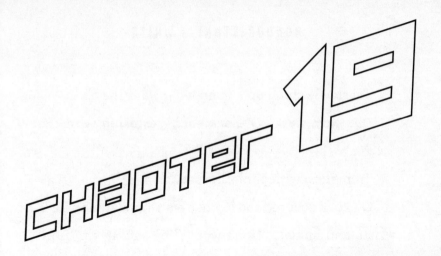

CHAPTER 19

11:52 P.M.

With the Sizzler still pointed at Taj, O'Clock stepped back to the corner of the room where a black sheet was draped over an old chair. When O'Clock pulled off the sheet, Taj realized it wasn't any old chair but an electric chair. The old wooden arms were splintered and the metal bolts were rusty, but it had clearly been updated. Glowing red sensors had been affixed to the head strap. A tangle of wires ran from the back to a handheld dial.

O'Clock pointed to the chair. "Have a seat."

Taj slowly stood up and edged toward the chair.

"Quickly, now," O'Clock said, gesturing with the Sizzler.

Trembling with panic, Taj sat down.

O'Clock secured the leather restraints around Taj's wrists and ankles. "Don't worry," he said in a syrupy voice. "The last thing I want to do is kill you. What use would you be to me then? I've modified this chair for a much greater purpose. Back when I was Father Time, I was famous for my inventions—scanners, High Beams, I even perfected freezing time. But this is my greatest achievement. You see, Taj, you may not be able to control your powers, but I can." He pulled the head strap down over Taj's forehead. "I call it a Time Warp." He picked up the dial and turned it on. There was a humming sound and the red lights began to glow. "Now I can return time to whomever I want. And guess who I've chosen? Me!"

Taj struggled against the restraints, but he couldn't move an inch. "Sounds pretty selfish," he glowered.

"SELFISH?!" O'Clock screamed. "You want to talk to me about selfish?! I squandered my life protecting greedy little time wasters like you! I slaved away at that Agency, defending time day in and day out. And how did you people choose to spend this precious time?! Shoving greasy pizzas in your mouths! Riding your bicycles around for no reason at all! Climbing trees even though you know there's *nothing at the top*! I bet there's nothing you'd rather be doing right now than lazing around with your friends watching TV and playing video games!" O'Clock spat on the ground. "Well, guess what? I've got a video game for you. Take a look at your district!"

He turned on the computer screens. Taj saw the familiar graph of the Timeline but now the glowing red dot hovered just above it.

"It's 11:56 PM," O'Clock said. "Four minutes until everyone you know is lost forever. The Agency would call it a tragedy. I call it progress. If people make the choice to waste their time, I'm going to take it and make use of it myself."

O'Clock turned the dial all the way up. All of the stolen summer time that was piled up in the middle of the room shot toward Taj so fast that he felt like he was in a sandstorm in the middle of the Sahara. The sensors on his forehead glowed blindingly bright. Taj became completely cocooned in sand, and his mind's eye was assaulted with images so vivid it felt like he was experiencing them in real time—water balloon wars on Crescent Street; the Fourth of July fireworks in the hilly park; the Gut Punch coaster at Hurly World; Zoe's face covered in ice cream—it all became real to Taj in one epic flash.

But then the fun swirled away like water down the tub drain and Taj was rocked by the horrifying image of O'Clock's face. It was so clear, so close-up Taj could count the wrinkled lines in his face. He could see every silver hair sprouting from his chin. He could read his pores like points on a map.

Taj's eyes snapped open. The sand warped toward

O'Clock. It looked like time itself was being held against its will as it traveled in an arc across the room. It enveloped O'Clock like a tornado then, all at once, it disappeared.

Taj slumped in the chair, exhausted.

O'Clock took a deep breath in and smiled. "Well done, Taj. We're off to an excellent start!"

"Start?" Taj rasped.

"Oh, yes, the work is just beginning! So much more fun time to steal!" O'Clock dashed over to the monitors. "Look! My scanner has just detected a new batch. Let's go get it, shall we?" He pressed a key on the control panel and Taj heard an alarm sounding throughout the prison. Then, through the window, he saw all of the time thieves flood out from the cellblocks and scurry off the island toward San Francisco.

O'Clock watched them go, a smug look on his face. "There's something so satisfying about a full circle, don't you think? The rotation of the Earth around the sun, the minute hand moving around the clock. And now, all the world's fun time traveling to me—so that I can live forever."

"An endless life without any fun? I'd rather be dead." Taj scowled.

O'Clock smirked. "Well, you don't have a choice, now, do you? All time belongs to me now."

Taj weakly wrestled against the restraints, but it was no use. It was 11:59. O'Clock had everyone's summers. There was nothing Taj could do. Syd was gone. Eon was dead. O'Clock had won.

But then Taj remembered that maybe he did have some of his own time left.

"Hey!" he shouted at O'Clock. "What about *my* summer? You said I could have it!"

"Oh yes!" O'Clock clapped his hands together. "How could I forget?" He walked behind the desk and with great effort, hoisted up a heavy jug of sand. "I said you could have it . . . *if* you behaved." He poured the sand out slowly in a circle around Taj. "And behave, you did not." He tossed the jug aside. "More for me."

He turned the dial.

Taj's summer shot up around him. The most fun time he had ever known flashed across the backs of his eyelids. Then, just as O'Clock's face appeared, Taj forced himself to open his eyes. He stared down at Eon and focused harder than he ever had in his entire life. His head rang with pain and his lungs felt like they might collapse, but he fought through it. He concentrated on Eon like he was the peach pit, like he was the only thing in the entire world.

And slowly, the time began to bend toward Eon.

"Wh—what's happening?!" said O'Clock.

"It's my time," Taj said through gritted teeth. "I get to choose how to spend it."

All at once, the sand rained down on Eon and disappeared. Eon sat up with a start, gasping, coughing like he'd been saved from drowning. He placed his hand over his chest where the blade had gone through, but it was completely healed. He looked up at Taj. "You . . . You gave me your summer to save my life."

Taj grinned. "You know what they say. Time heals all wounds."

"No!" O'Clock shouted, reaching for the Sizzler.

But Eon was already on his feet. He kicked O'Clock in the stomach, sending him crashing into the desk, toppling a bookcase onto him. Before O'Clock could dig out from under the piles of old books, Eon rushed over to Taj. He unstrapped him, yanking the wires out from the back of the head strap. A shower of sparks flew out and the bright red sensors went dark.

"My masterpiece!" O'Clock wailed. He dragged himself to the doorway and shouted, "HELP! HELP!"

"Your army is gone," said Taj. "You're all alone."

Eon began to move toward O'Clock, his fists clenched. But then they heard footsteps outside.

"Not *all* alone," O'Clock said.

The office door swung open and the Snoozer walked in.

"Where's Syd?!" said Taj.

The Snoozer's nostrils flared. "Left her for dead."

"Good boy," O'Clock said. "Kill them, too."

The Snoozer lunged at Eon and Taj, and with its enormous claw pinned them against the wall by their necks.

Out of the corner of his eye, Taj saw Syd hoist herself up through the window. Without making a sound, she grabbed the detonator from on top of the warden's desk.

"Left her for dead, huh?" Taj said. He looked at O'Clock. "Your bodyguard is tough … but not so smart."

Syd pushed the button on the detonator. The implant in the Snoozer's neck glowed red, and with a thunderous blast, it exploded into a thousand pieces.

O'Clock tried to make a run for it, but Eon grabbed him by the arms and turned him toward Taj.

"What are you going to do?" O'Clock spat. "I have the summers. You're too late."

Taj looked at the monitors. His district was about to collide with the Timeline. Ten seconds left.

"Actually," he said. "I'm just in time."

He locked eyes with O'Clock and focused so intensely he could see the tiny flecks of gold and brown in his irises. He felt charged like a magnet. He was in control. He was the Worm.

There was an earthshaking blast as the sand erupted out of O'Clock. But Taj stood firm. The summers spiraled around him with so much power that he felt like every molecule in his body was going to be pulled apart in different directions. He was in the eye of a time tornado. His body felt like it was on fire. And just as he couldn't take it anymore, the time shot upward, tearing a massive hole in the roof of Alcatraz and scattering across the night sky. And then, everything went black.

CHAPTER 20

7:35 A.M.

T aj! Wake up! You're going to be late for school!"
Taj heard his mom's voice and a familiar
pounding on his door. He shot up and rubbed
the sleep from his eyes. He was in his bedroom.

What happened?

He rushed downstairs. Everything was completely
normal. His mom was making pancakes and his dad
was sitting at the kitchen table, reading the newspaper.
Taj ripped it out of his hands to look at the front page.

"Good morning to you, too," Dad huffed.

Taj read the headline on the front page: TUESDAY SEPTEMBER 6.

"Good morning? Great morning!" Taj shouted then kissed his dad right on his shiny bald head.

Dad narrowed his eyes. "You sure are happy for the second day of school."

Just then Zoe padded into the kitchen. When she saw Taj, she jumped on him and shouted, "TAJ AT-TACK!"

"Zoe!" He lifted her in the air and looked up at her beaming face. "You're . . ." There were no words to describe just how happy he felt. ". . . awake!"

Mom sighed, "Taj, she's five years old. She's been awake for *hours*."

"Do the hamster! Do the hamster!" said Zoe.

Taj started to puff up his cheeks but then he thought of something. "In a minute. First, I'm going to do something I should have done a long time ago." He knelt down in front of her. "Want to learn how you tie your shoes?"

"Yes!" Zoe cheered.

Taj made a loop with one of the laces of her sparkly red sneakers. "Here's the bunny ear, okay?" Then he held up the other lace. "And here's the . . . hm." This was where he'd gotten stuck the last time. Sure, it was easy to tie your shoes once you knew how, but actually putting it into words was really difficult.

But this time, he was determined to keep going. "Here's the . . ." He stared at the outstretched lace. "Worm! It wiggles around the bunny ear then digs its little worm body under the ground." Taj wrapped the string around the loop. "Then you pull tight." He pulled, forming a perfect bow. "And the bunny has two ears, just like it's supposed to." He tapped Zoe's nose. "And *that's* how you keep from falling down when you're playing hopscotch."

Zoe tried the other shoe and made a lopsided bow.

"Don't worry," said Taj. "We'll practice more after school."

Mom smiled. "Thank you, Taj." Then her smile faded. "Now move your butt, buster. The bus is almost here."

|||||||||||||||||||||||||||||||||||||||||||||||||||||

When Taj got to the bus stop he found Jen and Lucas in a spirited debate. The first thing Taj noticed was that Jen was wearing matching socks. The second thing he noticed was the faint ring of maple syrup around Lucas's mouth.

"A hundred and fifty!" said Lucas.

"No way! Three hundred!" When Jen saw Taj she pointed at him and said, "You can settle this. How many balloons would it take to lift Lucas into the air?"

"How high?" Taj asked.

"High enough to drop a carton of eggs down Vice Principal Eggbert's chimney." Lucas giggled. "With a name like that, he's got it coming!"

At first, Taj didn't answer, he just grinned from ear to ear. Everything really was back to normal. "Five hundred *at least*," he said.

Jen punched Lucas in the arm. "Told ya!" Then she said thoughtfully, "It's going to be a true challenge to top the best summer ever."

"But we can try!" Lucas raised his eyebrows. "Only four more days till the weekend!"

Soon, the school bus arrived. "I call window seat!" Jen said, running up the steps. Lucas followed behind her.

Taj was about to step onboard when everything froze.

He looked hopefully up the street. Sure enough, there was the out-of-service bus. It stopped in front of him and the doors swung open.

Syd leaned out, holding a half-eaten candy bar. "You coming?"

Taj glanced at the school bus. As much as he wanted to be with his friends, he knew he was needed somewhere else. He climbed up the steps and saw Eon at the steering wheel. Same spotless gray suit. Same steely-eyed expression.

"Would it kill you to smile?" Taj said.

The corner of Eon's mouth turned upward ever so slightly.

"I'll take it," said Taj.

"F.T. wanted me to give you this," Eon said. He handed Taj a black watch identical to his own.

Taj fastened it around his wrist. The cold black metal felt heavier than he expected. The screen lit up with red text that said: Calibrating.

"This part stings," said Eon.

Taj's fingertips prickled with pain like they were being punctured by a thousand tiny needles. Blue scans of his fingerprints appeared on the watch face. There was a surge of electricity from his wrist to his heart. He staggered forward and Eon held out his hand to steady him.

Then there were two loud beeps. The watch screen said: Taj Carter—Time Tracer.

Taj pushed the red button on the side of the watch and time unfroze. He smiled. "Let's go have some fun."

ACKNOWLEDGMENTS

To our family, the reason time feels so precious.

To our friends, the reason time passes so quickly.

To Julien and Robbie, for the inspiration. And to their parents, Byron and Brandon, for your friendship.

To Jason Richman, for your guidance and for picking up the phone when we call.

To our mentor and beloved agent, Erica Silverman, for introducing us to your awesome husband, Jared.

To our editor, David Linker, who for some reason insisted that this story make sense. Thank you for your endless patience.

To Pizza, for always being there.

Also by
ANNABETH BONDOR-STONE
and
CONNOR WHITE!

Meet Shivers, the scaredy-est pirate
to ever sail the Seven Seas!

HARPER

An Imprint of HarperCollinsPublishers

www.harpercollinschildrens.com